To Michael
With Best Wishes
— Kirk

WILLIAM KILPATRICK

A POST HILL PRESS book

ISBN (Trade Paperback): 978-1-61868-943-6
ISBN (eBook): 978-1-61868-944-3

Cover art by Matthew J. Mosley

This book is a work of fiction. People, places, events, and situations are the product of the author's imagination. Any resemblance to actual persons, living or dead, or historical events, is purely coincidental.

CHAPTER 1

On a table to one side of the darkened room lay a suitcase-sized crate stenciled with several "biohazard" warnings.

With a few deft strokes of a small crowbar, Colonel Mohammed Faisal pried off the top. Inside, carefully packed in foam, were eight steel cylinders, each about the size of a thermos and each printed with similar warning labels.

Faisal carefully removed one of the cylinders and displayed it to the four other men in the room who were gathered around the table and were dressed, like him, in military uniforms.

"This is what we've been waiting for," said the colonel in perfect English. "A fraction of a drop is enough to kill a man instantaneously. A few of these containers introduced into the water supply of a large city – such as Washington – will result in widespread death and panic."

The others, all of Middle-Eastern appearance, responded with murmurs of approval.

Faisal continued. "But let's hope we don't have to use it. I have no desire to cause needless suffering. We have other means of persuasion that should be sufficient. If not, this is our backup." He paused. "One other thing. Zero Day has been moved up to the tenth."

"But Colonel," complained a younger officer, "that only

gives us four days."

"That surprises you? Good. It will come as much more of a surprise to our friends in Washington. Less time for us to get ready? Perhaps. But, more importantly, less time for them to discover our plans. Any questions?"

"Is there any danger of the chemical leaking beforehand?" asked a short, doleful-looking officer with a drooping mustache. This was Major Osman Osama, the second in command.

"No danger at all. Here, take a closer look." And with that, Faisal casually tossed the cylinder to the major. The container was not heavy, but Osama's knees buckled as he caught it and his face turned pale. The other officers jumped back, shielding their faces as they retreated.

"Calm down," said Faisal with an amused smile. "The chemical is inert until the activator agent is added."

Major Osama let out his breath and shook his head reproachfully. "Colonel, you shouldn't joke like that. Our nerves are already on edge."

"Yes, you're right, Major," admitted Faisal. "My apologies. We will save the jokes for later."

"But where is this activator agent?" asked Major Osama.

"It will arrive tomorrow," replied the colonel. "In fact, my wife will deliver it."

"But what about security? Won't they search the car?"

"You worry too much, Major. She will have it hidden where no one will dare to look for it."

CHAPTER 2

The main entrance to Fort Camp is approached by a three-mile road that winds through meadows and woods and ends at a gatehouse. Fifty feet short of the gatehouse a large sign proclaims: "WELCOME TO FORT CAMP: THE PROUD, THE BRAVE, THE PRECIOUS FEW."

At ten-thirty on a Tuesday morning, a black late-model SUV pulled to a stop at the gate. A uniformed soldier stepped out of the narrow gatehouse and peered into the open window of the car. Inside were two women dressed in black burqas. At least, Sergeant Cooper was pretty sure they were women, even though all he could see was their eyes.

"Is that you, Mrs. Faisal?" he inquired of the driver. She nodded her head. Looking over to the passenger he asked, "Mrs. Faisal?" The passenger also nodded her head.

"Well, look ladies," said Sergeant Cooper with a slight drawl that didn't manage to hide the discomfort he was feeling, "you know you're not supposed to wear those get-ups when you come through security. How am I supposed to identify you?"

The driver helpfully handed over an ID card.

"Well, Mrs. Faisal, you know I got to see your face

too. Would you mind removing that head covering? This is supposed to be a high-security base."

The putative Mrs. Faisal firmly shook her head in the negative. So did the other Mrs. Faisal.

"Ladies, you're putting me in a bad spot. Regulations say I have to check everyone's identity."

The first Mrs. Faisal murmured some words under her veil which had the effect of producing a more worried look on Sgt. Cooper's already tense face.

"I know Colonel Faisal would be angry if he found out," he admitted.

She murmured a few more muffled words.

"Yeah, I guess General Coddle wouldn't be too happy either. Well, shoot! Would you promise me you are who you are? You wouldn't lie to me about a thing like that? Would you?"

Both Mrs. Faisals shook their heads in the negative.

"Cross your heart and swear to God? ...I mean swear to Allah? Well, you don't have to cross your heart either. I mean if you would just nod, that ought to be good enough."

The two women nodded slightly.

"Okay," said Sgt. Cooper waving them through and shaking his head in wonderment, "I'll let it go this time. You sure make my job awful hard."

CHAPTER 3

About a half-mile back on the same entrance road, another car approached the gate. Seated in the back, Captain James Cassandra, age thirty-four, surveyed the pleasant scenery and congratulated himself on his new assignment. Alaska had been a challenge. It had provided him an opportunity to put his skills to good use and had earned him a promotion as well, but it was time for a change. He was proud of his service at his previous post, but glad to be, at last, in less isolated environs.

At the gate, the driver who had met him at the airport exchanged some banter with the guard on duty. The guard appeared excessively relieved to see a familiar face. As is sometimes the case with those who have recently gone through a trying experience, he seemed anxious to talk. Understandably, however, he could not talk about what was really on his mind. After some minutes of this superfluous chatter, the car, to Cassandra's relief, moved on and brought him within a few minutes to a square three story building marked "Headquarters."

Before exiting the car, Cassandra thanked the driver and received assurances that his luggage would be deposited at his new quarters. That done, he stepped out, pulled down on the hem of his neatly pressed uniform and turned to face the headquarters and what he hoped would be a new and interesting chapter in his life.

He was not disappointed. As he went up the steps he passed a pretty female private coming down. To his surprise, she cast him a come-on look. Flustered, he responded with a nod and an awkward smile. Fort Camp was not quite what he expected. Captain Cassandra appreciated the female form as much as the next man, but he was still a bit old-school about such matters. According to protocol, privates weren't supposed to flirt with captains. Nevertheless, in a moment of weakness he glanced back at the shapely soldier as she descended the steps.

As he did so, the toe of his shoe caught on the topmost step and sent him catapulting through the still-open doors of the headquarters and into a hefty, short-cropped female sergeant, causing her to drop an armful of folders.

"Sorry, sorry," he mumbled as he squatted down to gather up the folders.

The sergeant, whose eyes were not nearly as soft as the private's, simply glared at him with ill-concealed contempt. Cassandra, who, because of his name, knew something of mythology, felt he had suddenly passed from the presence of Aphrodite into the clutches of Medusa – if indeed there could be such a creature as a short-cropped Medusa. Apologizing once again, he handed back the folders to the still-silent sergeant and cast his eyes about looking for some way to extricate himself from the situation.

CHAPTER 4

At that moment a dark-haired officer who looked to be in his late twenties came to the rescue.

"Captain Cassandra? I'm Lieutenant Lopez. Welcome to Fort Camp," he said, holding out his hand.

"Thanks. Nice to meet you," replied the still- flustered Captain. Not knowing what else to say, he added, "Seems like a well-run place you have here."

"Thanks. We try our best. Let me show you your new office. It's right over here."

Lieutenant Lopez, who seemed eager to please, led the way through the open-area desks and over to a private office – one of several that lined the far side of the room.

"This used to be Captain Jessup's office," he said as he opened the door. "I think you'll find everything in order."

"It looks fine," replied Cassandra, "a lot better than my old place."

"I hear you were in Alaska, sir."

"Yes, three cold years in the tundra. How about yourself? Have you been here long?"

"Oh, about three years."

"And before that? Judging from all those ribbons on your chest, you must have seen some action."

"Not really, sir. I've been pretty much a desk jockey. Actually these are non-combat badges."

Non-combat or not, Lopez's voice betrayed a hint of pride as he pointed to his badges. "This one is for completion of the inclusiveness program. This one's for anger management, and this one's for sensitivity under stress. Oh, and this one's for pride. But all the officers here automatically get that one."

To Cassandra, who had seen combat, this seemed much ado about nothing, but he was too polite to let it show.

"Oh, I see. How about this Captain Jessup? What happened to him?"

"He took early retirement. I think he had a hard time adjusting to all the changes to the base. He used to have an American flag on the wall over there. General Coddle

made him take it down. Said it was insensitive to minorities. I think that was the last straw for Captain Jessup."

This revelation was a bit disconcerting for Cassandra, but he managed to make a joke of it.

"Really?... Well, that's no problem for me. I developed a lot of sensitivity in Alaska – sensitivity to the cold, mainly."

Lieutenant Lopez chuckled.

"So, have there been many of these changes?" asked Cassandra.

"Oh, a few. General Coddle says that society is always evolving, so the Army has to evolve to keep up."

Looking out the open office door, Cassandra spotted a tall bearded officer exiting another office. Cassandra, who was quick to notice such things, observed that the officer's shoulder patch featured two crossed scimitars and what appeared to be a book.

"Hey, what sort of patch is that officer wearing? It doesn't look like any sensitivity badge."

"Oh, that's the emblem of the Muslim

Brotherhood. It's a fraternal organization – sort of like the Shriners, I think."

"And how come he's wearing a beard? I thought beards were against regulations."

"Well, yes and no. Ordinarily, yes, but there's an exemption for Muslims. That's Lieutenant Jabar. I'll introduce you to him later. Meanwhile, General Coddle has asked me to give you a tour of the base."

CHAPTER 5

Fort Camp was considerably larger than Cassandra's previous post in Alaska. In fact, it was essentially a large town, complete with a supermarket, movie theater, tennis courts, swimming pool, elementary school, and suburban type townhouses and single family homes for officers and their families. If it weren't for the occasional bearded officer, it would have been the picture of normalcy. There was one other discordant note, however; Cassandra saw that the signs were posted not only in English and Spanish but also in Arabic.

Surely that isn't necessary, he thought. Probably just a SOP to appease the politically correct. He was brought out of his reflection by Lieutenant Lopez who was cheerfully pointing out the sights.

"Here's the gas station. If you need to fill'er up, just use your base credit card."

The gas pumps were painted a sky blue color and featured a corn stalk emblem. The price placards above read:

Regular: $28.50
Premium: $30.00
Diesel: $32.50

"I see someone's been joking around with the prices," said Cassandra with a smile.

"Oh, that's no joke, sir," said Lopez earnestly, "All the services use special bio-friendly fuel now. It's a little more expensive, but it keeps the environment clean."

"Thirty dollars a gallon! But back on the highway it was less than four!"

"Army regulations says we can only gas up on the base.

Don't worry, sir, the Army's cutting back in other areas – less troops, fewer tanks and humvees. So, it all evens out."

Cassandra was all for giving the environment its due, but he couldn't help wondering what bank account the army was padding by paying these exorbitant prices. It would be nice to be on the other end of that thirty-dollar-a-gallon transaction.

"Hmmm...well, I suppose it encourages more walking. There's something to be said for doing things the ooold..."

His voice trailed off as he beheld two handsome soldiers of the male sex walking toward them. They were holding hands and exchanging fond glances. Cassandra's head turned as they passed by.

"...the old fashioned way," he finished lamely.

When Lt. Lopez who hadn't noticed anything amiss and hadn't slackened his pace, saw that Cassandra had fallen behind, he beckoned to him.

"Over this way, Captain."

Cassandra quickened his pace but his thoughts remained behind. What sort of place had he landed in? He knew, of course, about the new policy that had replaced "Don't Ask Don't Tell," but he didn't believe it allowed for this sort of fraternizing. Before he could complete his thoughts, however, another sight met his eyes which prompted an entirely different chain of thought.

Coming round a curve in the walk were three morbidly obese soldiers. The buttons on their shirts could scarcely contain their bulk and ovals of white T-shirt peeped through their khaki colored uniforms at intervals between each button. They looked, thought Cassandra, like three well-fed ducks. How, he wondered, did they ever make it through basic training? For that matter, how had they made it past the recruitment officer's desk? He cast a disapproving look in their direction as they waddled by.

"Shouldn't they be put on a diet?"

Lopez seemed a bit surprised. "Uh, no, sir, that would be weightism."

"Weightism?"

"Discrimination on the basis of weight or size. It's part of the new regs."

Cassandra raised his eyebrows. "Hmmm, maybe..."

He was going to make a joke about the overweight soldiers serving as replacements for the cancelled tanks and humvees, but he thought better of it. It occurred to him that the new regs might have something to say about insensitive jokes as well.

"Yes, sir?"

"Oh, nothing, nothing. Where to next?"

"Thought you might like to see the base housing."

CHAPTER 6

"This is the housing for non-Muslim families," said Lopez as they approached a neighborhood of neat but look-alike town houses. "The Muslim section is over there. We hoped everyone would assimilate, but it hasn't worked out that way. I'll show you around."

As they walked up the closest street, they made their way around boys and girls playing hopscotch, jump rope, and other innocuous games. Cassandra didn't particularly approve of boys playing jump rope together with girls. He had always thought of it as essentially a girl's game. But he grudgingly admitted to himself that he had grown up in a different era. Of course, it wasn't that long ago that he had been a boy himself, but in that short interval the gender busybodies had managed to insert themselves into every social nook and cranny.

The two stopped for a while to observe the play. "Well," thought Cassandra to himself, "They're having fun. Who am I to judge?"

A worried-looking mother who was standing nearby called out to one of the boys playing hopscotch. "Billy, please be careful. You might hurt yourself."

Billy, whose gender conditioning did not seem quite complete, paid no attention, but Lieutenant Lopez was impressed with the mother's caution. Turning to

Cassandra, he said, "Can't be too careful. I sprained my ankle once doing that."

After a suitable time surveying this slice of suburbia, the two officers headed over to the Muslim housing section. Unlike "Pleasantville" (as Cassandra thought of the neighborhood they had just visited), the Muslim area was surrounded by a high chain link fence. And on the fence a large yellow sign proclaimed: "YOU ARE ENTERING A SHARIA CONTROLLED ZONE." Below the warning were a number of circle-backslash symbols indicating that drinking was prohibited, along with drugs, dancing, short skirts, gambling, and music. Cassandra himself was no advocate for loose living, but he thought this was going too far. It was a bit of brazen chutzpah – if, indeed, there could be such a thing as Islamic *chutzpah*. He wondered if it might be a hate crime to put the two words together.

At the gate, a bearded guard allowed them to pass through. The townhouses were not very different from those in the other neighborhood, but there was a distinct smell of spices and other cooking odors in the air. The first jarring note was the children. There were no boys and girls playing together – only boys. The girls must have been hidden inside the houses. And the boys were not playing in any traditional sense. They were dressed in mujahideen outfits and wore the green and white martyr's bandanna around their heads. Under the watchful eyes of a few burqa-clad mothers, the boys were playing serious war games, including bayonet practice (albeit with wooden bayonets) and hand-to-hand combat. Young as they were, the Muslim boys were already highly accomplished in martial arts. Cassandra looked on in amazement.

At that point, a Muslim officer came out of a nearby townhouse and spoke in a low voice to one of the older boys.

"Go inside now and work on your last testament

video."

The boy bowed obediently and went inside.

Since the father spoke in Arabic, Cassandra and Lopez could only surmise what he said. Lopez, who was always willing to put the best face on things, saw nothing more than a tight-knit traditional family functioning as it should.

"You know," he said, "it's really great to see a dad take an interest in his son like that."

Cassandra, who was a bit more dubious, could only reply, "Uh, right. I was just thinking the same thing."

Further down and out of sight of the main gate, a trio of Muslim soldiers was gathered on the stoop of one of the houses. Two of them were carrying holstered weapons, and the third was inspecting his service pistol. They were speaking in Arabic.

"Why bother with a martyr's video?" said the tallest of the three. "This is not a martyrdom operation. If you have any doubts, wear Kevlar."

"Or make sure your Kalashnikov is well-oiled," chimed in a second soldier who was seated on the stoop.

"Okay, okay, but no plan's perfect," replied the third – the one who was inspecting his weapon.

Noticing the approach of two officers, the tall soldier alerted his companions. "Better change the subject—and the language."

The seated soldier caught on quickly. Speaking in English and in a voice the passersby couldn't help but hear, he enthused, "Did you see that Phillies game last night?"

"Yeah, that was a close one!" said the third, trying to imitate the ardor of a true sports enthusiast.

"How about that homer by Fernandez in the top of the third? Man, that guy can hit!" The tall soldier, who actually was a Phillies fan, was sure they had given the right impression.

Cassandra, however, was skeptical by nature. He

had been observing the trio from a distance and quickly sensed that something was not right. After he and Lopez had passed by, the soldiers resumed their conversation in Arabic, being careful to speak in more hushed tones. With a quizzical look, Cassandra glanced back at them over his shoulder, then turned to Lopez.

"Did you see that? They're carrying weapons. Only MPs are supposed to be armed on base. What gives?"

"That rule's been changed, sir. Muslim soldiers are allowed to carry now. It's a gesture of trust. The General says that trust is an important concept in their culture."

"Gesture of trust! Next thing they'll be giving F-16s to the Iranian Air Force. That would be a gesture of trust, too."

"But sir! We *are* sending F-16s to Iran. It was just announced this morning."

"Just for peaceful purposes, I suppose?"

"Why, yes, sir!" said Lopez in surprise. "How did you know?"

"Oh, just a guess."

The tour of the base continued for another half hour and ended outside Cassandra's new quarters.

"Here's your quarters, sir."

"Thanks. Uh…just out of curiosity, do you know how many Muslim soldiers are on the base?"

"Can't say for sure. The General says we're all one family, and it would be divisive to count by race or religion. But between you and me, I'd say about 15 to 20 percent. And I notice the Muslim officers rise up in the ranks pretty fast. Well, I have to get back. You'll meet with General Coddle in the morning. By the way, there's a movie on the base tonight, if you'd like some entertainment."

"Thanks, I think I might. And thanks for the tour. By the way, where do I find the movie?"

"It's right down that way – the Harvey Milk Auditorium.

You can't miss it."

CHAPTER 7

The lobby of the base theater had a campy ambiance – perhaps in honor of the featured film, *Cabaret*. A sign over the refreshment stand read "KIT KAT KLUB." A young woman in a cigarette girl's outfit who was carrying a tray of cigarettes and sweets approached Cassandra. Or was it a woman? The make-up seemed excessive, and the voice a bit husky. Cassandra could no longer be sure of anything.

"Wilkommen, Mein Herr. Can I interest you in some cigarettes? Some candy?" It was not the best Marlene Dietrich impersonation, but it was a good try.

"Oh, no thanks, I think I'm late for the movie." replied the embarrassed captain. "Thanks anyway."

He moved quickly into the auditorium and took a seat near the front just as the opening scene of "Cabaret" played on the screen. It was not his favorite movie – too many risqué scenes for his taste. On the other hand, he had to admit that it did a good job of showing how a determined group of true believers could transform a country. What had started as little more than a cult, soon controlled the whole culture. It had only taken a half-dozen years to get the Germans accustomed to ideas that would have seemed insane or criminal to previous generations.

As he was musing on the collapse of civilizations, he felt a slight pressure on his left leg. Then, increasing pressure. Then, an up-and-down motion. The officer next to him was rubbing his knee against Cassandra's. When he glanced over, the officer, a good-looking man about his own age, gave him a certain kind of look with a very plain intent. To say that Cassandra was distressed would be to put it mildly. Nevertheless, he decided that an angry rejection of the man's advances was not called for. Maybe this was the normal form of introduction around here – like Eskimos in the arctic offering their wives to newly arrived guests.

He stood up and mumbled an apology. "Excuse me. Just need to use the men's room."

This, thought Cassandra, would fool the man into thinking he would return. He had no such intention, of course. His plan was to leave the theater immediately. The officer, however, mistook Cassandra's intention entirely. As the captain walked back up the aisle, the other man followed. Apparently, a rendezvous in the men's room was just what he desired.

Now thoroughly distressed, Cassandra quickened his pace, pushed past some late arrivals coming down the aisle, and rushed into the lobby where he nearly knocked over the startled cigarette boy/girl. Before his fellow officer had even made it to the lobby, Cassandra was outside. Thankful for the darkness, he quickly left his puzzled pursuer far behind.

CHAPTER 8

As he wandered through the dimly lit town, Cassandra passed fraternizing soldiers of both sexes and possibly of sexual orientations yet to be discovered. Shortly after, he came to a building with a lighted sign. It read. "Officers' Club."

The club was empty except for the barman, a dark-skinned jolly fellow who wore a white jacket and a white turban and spoke with a Pakistani accent. Though partly concealed by the turban, a slight bump was visible in the center of the man's forehead.

"How may I serve you, sir?" he asked cheerfully.

"Oh. I guess I'll have a scotch and water."

"I am very sorry, sir. We no longer serve alcohol."

"What! Why not?"

"It is *haram*, sir."

"Harem? You mean like a bunch of kept women?"

The bartender smiled. "No, no. Not 'harem.' '*Haram.*' *Haram* is an Arabic term. It means 'forbidden'." His smile broadened. "Perhaps someday, if Allah wills, we will have the harem, too. However, right now I can offer you some very fine Arabic coffee."

"No, no. I'm a little too jittery for that. Thanks anyway."

"As Allah wishes," replied the bartender with an enigmatic smile.

Cassandra needed a drink more than he needed to discuss the niceties of the Arabic language, so he thanked the barman again and headed for the door.

CHAPTER 9

Cassandra entered his quarters, talking to himself.

"No whiskey, huh. Hmm, let's see what we have here."

He opened the liquor cabinet, which Lopez had thoughtfully stocked with a few bottles.

"Here we go."

He pulled out a bottle of whiskey, poured a glass, and started to sip.

"Ahh! *Haram* be damned."

After a while, he put down the glass, pulled out his cell phone, and punched in a number.

"Hello, Larry? It's Jim Cassandra."

"Long time, no see," said Larry. "How are things?"

"Oh, pretty good. I just got reassigned from Alaska to Fort Camp, and I thought I'd call to touch bases – no pun intended."

"What's the pun?"

"Well, you're at a base and I'm at a base, and we're in touch by phone. So we're touching bases. Get it?"

"Yeah, I get it, but I'd say it was more of a ground-out than a base hit. Get it? *Base hit*."

"Touché."

"So, how do you like Fort Camp?"

"Well, it's different – kind of strange, actually: like

Provincetown and Mecca all mixed together, if you know what I mean."

"Tell me about it. It's the same here – only more like Mecca."

"Hmm. How about the other bases in the area?"

"Same all over, from what I hear."

"Well, how about Fort Blister? General Mandrake runs a pretty tight ship, doesn't he?"

"He's been replaced – with a Muslim commandant."

"You're kidding me, right?"

"Nope. But I think you're reading too much into it. The army's just trying to reach out to minorities. Don't tell me you're getting prejudiced in your old age."

"Okay, okay, I'm beginning to sound like a homophobic Islamophobe, but you know me better than that. It just seems odd, that's all."

"You're the one who's going to seem odd if you start pedaling conspiracy theories. Are you sure you're getting enough sleep?"

"Well, to tell the truth, I am feeling some jet lag. I wasn't able to sleep much on the plane. Anyway, thanks for the input. I have to sign off now but, uh, let's keep in touch.

"Let's do that. Take care."

"You too. Bye."

He put down the cell phone and reflected on what he had just heard. *Conspiracy theories.* Everyone brushed them aside as a joke. On the other hand, *not every conspiracy is a theory.* The words came back to him from something he had seen years ago on television – a commercial advertising some spy/thriller series. A cheap advertising trick, perhaps, but it contained an element of truth. After all, there had been plenty of real conspiracies. History was full of them.

Maybe I just need some sleep? *Or maybe it's time to wake up.*

CHAPTER 10

The next morning, Captain Cassandra dropped in on Lieutenant Lopez before his meeting with General Coddle. Lopez was sitting at his desk, looking at his laptop screen. He seemed perturbed.

"Darn!"

"What's the trouble?"

"It's this darned dating service I signed up for. They don't pay any attention to the preferences I put down."

"What do you mean?"

"Well, for example, I'm a Catholic, and I'd like to meet a Catholic girl, but they keep matching me with Hindus and Unitarians and even atheists. Ever since the dating services were nationalized, they put in this new set of nondiscrimination rules. So if you want to date someone of your own religion, you're discriminating against all the others. Can you beat that?"

"Hmm. Sounds like Big Brother is matching you."

"Big Brother?"

"Yes, from *1984*."

"1984?"

"It's a book written in 1948 about 1984."

"Why would they write a book about 1984 in 1948?"

"Well, the author wanted to show how a society could control a person's thoughts and emotions, and...well, never mind. Look, instead of a dating service, why don't you try your luck with the women on the base? There seem to be plenty of them."

"Believe me, I have. Trouble is, most of the women on base aren't interested in men."

"Oh, yeah, I see. Well, I hope your luck changes, Lieutenant, but right now I have an appointment with General Coddle. I'd better not keep him waiting. Where do I find his office?"

"Down the hall and to your right, sir."

CHAPTER 11

General Coddle occupied a large, well-appointed office in the corner of the building. It contained several upholstered leather chairs, a sofa, and a mahogany desk behind which at the moment sat a slightly plump, red-cheeked man who appeared to be in his mid-fifties. Coddle wore a genial expression and a casual open-collar uniform without a jacket. Cassandra noted a large "COEXIST" poster on the wall behind the desk.

As he entered, General Coddle waved him in, rose from his desk, and extended a plump hand.

"Welcome, Captain. Don't bother to salute. We don't stand on formalities here. I understand you were last stationed in Alaska?" As he said this, he clasped Cassandra's hand with both of his own and began to pump vigorously.

"Er... yes," said Cassandra uncomfortably, "a rather remote part of Alaska – a bit secluded, you know."

"Ah, yes. Well, how are you getting on here?"

"Well, sir, it's a little different from what I'm used to, but I'm sure I'll adjust."

Coddle, who was still holding Cassandra's hand, offered some reassurance.

"I'm sure you will, my boy, and if you have any trouble adjusting, we have some very good people in the

Behavioral Health Unit."

"Oh, I think I'll be all right. There's just one thing, though…"

At this point, Coddle released Cassandra's hand and threw a fatherly arm around his shoulder.

"Feel free to share anything that's on your mind, Captain. We're not judgmental around here."

"Well, sir, I've noticed that there are an awful lot of Muslim soldiers and officers on the base. It just seems a bit strange, you know."

"Jim… you don't mind if I call you Jim? What you see is the result of our 'Proud to Be Me' program."

"Proud to be me?"

"Yes. It's the Army's new affirmative-action program for Muslims and gays – the two most under-represented minorities in the military."

"They don't seem so underrepresented now, sir."

Coddle released his hold on Cassandra, beamed proudly, and gestured with his hands for emphasis.

"That's true, that's true. And I'm very proud of the fact. You see, we're trying to make up for years of neglect."

"But I thought Muslims hated gays. Wouldn't that just create a lot of friction?"

"That's a common misunderstanding of Islam, Jim. In reality, our Muslim boys are about the most tolerant, accepting people I know. I believe their religion requires them to reach out to others."

"No, I guess I didn't realize that. Still, is it wise to bring so many Muslims so quickly onto our bases? I'm just thinking of what happened at Fort Hood, sir."

"On the contrary, Jim," said Coddle, speaking as would a kindly teacher to a not-so-bright student. "The lesson we learned from Fort Hood is that we need more Muslims in the military. Our behavioral experts determined that Major Hasan was a lone wolf who couldn't find the support and understanding he needed. There simply weren't enough fellow Muslims around to steer him straight. If our affirmative action strategy was in place then, that tragedy could have been averted. That's the lesson of Fort Hood, Jim."

"I see. Still, it concerns me that the Muslim officers here keep to themselves so much. Yesterday, I passed a group of soldiers who were speaking in Arabic. When I approached, they switched to English, and I also think they switched the topic of conversation. It looked like they were up to no good, General."

"That's not likely, Jim. Islam is a peaceful religion. You probably misinterpreted their behavior. We think they're talking subversion, and what they're actually doing is exchanging recipes for roast lamb. I think you'll find that once you get to know our men here, you'll see that there's nothing to be concerned about."

Captain Cassandra was unconvinced, but he thought it better not to pursue the matter any further.

"Well, I suppose you're right, General. I'll try to look on the bright side."

At that moment he spotted a framed photo on the General's desk which gave him an opportunity to change the subject.

"Say, that's a handsome young man. Your son, General?"

"No, I'm not married, Captain. Kenneth is just a very dear friend. I'll introduce you to him sometime."

"Oh, yes...yes, I hope we can meet, er...sometime. Well, sir, if there's nothing else, I'd better start catching up on my work."

"No, Jim, that's all. Pleasure to meet you. And don't forget, the Behavioral Health Unit is open twenty-four hours if you feel you need it." And with that he patted Cassandra on the back and guided him to the door.

CHAPTER 12

Watching through the window of the building they had surreptitiously converted into their command center, two Muslim officers observed Cassandra leaving the headquarters building. Colonel Mohammed Faisal was in his late thirties and wore a smartly tailored uniform and a neatly trimmed mustache. Tall and handsome and with charm to match, he might have been a movie star playing the role of a colonel. Major Osman Osama was about the same age, but he was shorter and wore an ill-fitting uniform. His heavy mustache was not groomed and, in contrast to the colonel, he wore a look of perpetual anxiety on his face.

"You think he knows anything, Colonel?"

"No, but it's best to play it safe. We'll need to keep an eye on him."

In another part of the room, Lieutenant Jabar, a gangly, bearded man with a toothy smile and protruding eyes was laughing and joking with another soldier. Colonel Faisal beckoned to him.

"Lieutenant Jabar, come here for a moment.... Do you see that officer?" He pointed to Cassandra. "I want you to follow him. See where he goes, who he talks to. Find out what you can about him – without raising suspicions. Then report to Major Osama here."

"Yes, sir."

"By the way, what were you laughing at just now?"

Jabar's face fell. "Uh... I just heard a new joke."

"And what is the joke?"

"Oh, it's not really so funny," he said nervously.

"Don't worry so much, Lieutenant. We all like to share in a good joke. You wouldn't want to leave us in suspense, would you?"

Lieutenant Jabar relaxed a bit after receiving this encouragement. "Uh... well... okay." He paused for effect, then delivered the set-up question with enthusiasm.

"What do you get when you burn a Koran?"

"I give up. What do you get when you burn a Koran?" replied Faisal coolly.

Jabar chuckled as he delivered the punch line.

"Holy smoke! Get it? – *holy smoke*."

"Yes, I get it, but I'm not sure you get it. So you think that is funny?" There was no mistaking the disapproval in Faisal's voice.

Jabar's smile faded quickly. "Oh, no sir, no. I was just repeating what I heard. I meant no disrespect, sir."

Luckily for Jabar, Major Osama who had more tolerance for human foibles, intervened with a quotation from the Ayatollah Khomeini that had the effect of putting an end to the nascent inquisition.

"There are no jokes in Islam, Lieutenant. Please try to remember that."

"Yes sir, sorry sir," said Jabar.

Colonel Faisal, who seemed to be satisfied that enough had been said, tossed his head toward the door and reissued his instruction to Jabar. "Go, do as I told you!"

"Yes, sir."

Relieved to be off the hook, Jabar quickly left the room. Colonel Faisal turned back to Major Osama.

"Perhaps someone should keep an eye on *him* before

he does something stupid.... So, Major, how is the plan progressing?"

"Just as you ordered, Colonel. But are you sure your information on the other bases is accurate?"

"I'll know more this afternoon – after I've talked with my little friend."

CHAPTER 13

In the base communications center, Private First Class Stanley Darling, a boyish-looking twenty-year-old was gossiping with other gay soldiers when Colonel Faisal entered. The group broke up as Faisal approached.

"Good afternoon, Private Darling," he said. "I apologize for scaring away your friends."

"Oh, don't worry about that, sir, they have work to do anyway. I've got that information you requested, Colonel. It's on this flash drive. I hope it's useful. I had to bend the rules to get it."

Bending the rules was easier to do when it was done in the service of someone like Colonel Faisal. As he handed over the flash drive, the look on Darling's face suggested that he was the one being favored. In truth, he had a crush on the handsome Colonel. Faisal replied in his smoothest voice.

"It will be very useful, Stanley – may I call you Stanley? I wish I could tell you what it concerns, but it is something that I need to keep under wraps for now. Let's just say that we're trying to investigate a case of discrimination."

"I just can't understand why people want to discriminate. It's so hateful." Darling spoke with becoming earnestness.

"Yes, your people have suffered much discrimination, and my people too. Homophobia, Islamophobia. They are just two sides of the same coin. We have much in common, you and I."

"I've always felt a lot in common with you, sir. I know that Muslims have suffered a lot for their beliefs.... And sir, I've never believed those stories about Muslims hating gays. I can see you're not like that."

Faisal wondered how he had ever allowed himself to be put in such a situation with this perverted puppy, but he didn't let his feelings interfere with his duty.

"Of course not. I'm glad to see you don't believe everything you hear. Unfortunately, they tell lies about our faith. Well, you would understand that. After all, they used to tell lies about the gays, also."

"They'd better not lie about us anymore. We've got power now."

"Yes, you do, Stanley. But be careful how you use it. Remember, with great power comes great responsibility."

"I never thought of it that way. I'll try to remember that...Sir?"

"Yes?"

"Do you think we could be friends?"

"But we already are friends."

Hopefully. "Well, what I mean is..."

Colonel Faisal knew very well what Darling meant, but he did his best to hide his discomfort.

"Oh, I see. Well, that is possible, Stanley, that is possible. But you must understand that I am a married man. In fact, I have two wives. I am not exactly free to do the things that I would like to do. You must give me time to think it over."

"Oh yes sir, of course! I know you're in a difficult situation. I can always hope that maybe someday..."

Faisal felt his jaw tense. "Well, perhaps that day is not too far off. In fact, I am sure the day will soon be here when I can openly express my real feelings toward you. There are so many ways in which I would like to express them."

Faisal realized that if he continued in this vein, his irony might become apparent even to this doe-eyed adolescent, so he suddenly adopted a less serious tone.

"But for now, business is business. I have a meeting to attend."

He turned to go and then, almost as an afterthought, he produced a slip of paper from his pocket and passed it to Darling.

"Oh, and here is one more bit of information I need for my project. It would be very helpful to our anti-discrimination campaign if you can obtain it."

"You can count on me, sir!"

"Thank you, Stanley, I know I can."

He had played his part well. Thank Allah, he would not have to play it much longer.

CHAPTER 14

Just as Colonel Faisal was leaving the building, Captain Cassandra entered. The two exchanged suspicious glances as they passed. As he approached the young private behind the desk, Cassandra wondered how one so innocent- looking had been placed in such a sensitive area as communications.

"Hello, sir. Can I help you?"

"Oh, yes. I'm Captain James Cassandra. I'm new to the base. Just trying to familiarize myself with the place. Are you the officer in charge here?" He knew, of course, that this was highly unlikely.

"Oh, no, sir. I'm just a private – Private Stanley Darling."

"Oh, is that so? Well, you could have fooled me. You have that look of command that one sees in officers. Do you serve under Colonel Faisal?"

"Not yet, sir, but I hope to soon."

"Yes, I see," said Cassandra in a knowing tone that was lost on the private. "Well, Darling, I wouldn't be surprised if they do put you in charge one of these days."

Darling brightened.

"That's nice of you to say so, sir. I do hope to move up in the ranks."

"Well, if I get the chance I'll put in a good word for

you. You remind me of my nephew. Handsome young man. Smart, too. He's a lieutenant already. Say, you must be pretty smart also to be able to handle all this electronic equipment."

"It does get complicated sometimes. I went to a special army school for training."

"Really? Say, tell me, do you have any of those new listening devices? The ones that let you hear conversations from a distance?"

"We have a few in stock."

"You don't suppose I could borrow one? It would be a big favor."

"I don't know, sir. They're supposed to be restricted."

"Sure, I understand. You have to go by the rules. But it would just be for a short time. You see, there are these damned mice behind the wall of my quarters, and they're driving me crazy at night with their scratching."

"Wow, that must be annoying!"

"If I could use that device I could locate exactly where they are, and then I could inject some rat poison in just the right place. Then, goodbye mice! And I'd finally be able to get some sleep. Of course, I don't want to put you on the spot…"

"Well, in that case, I guess it would be all right. Just don't tell anyone, or I'll get in trouble."

"Mum's the word."

Private Darling retrieved a package from a nearby shelf and handed it to Cassandra.

"Here it is, sir. The instructions are inside. By the way, since you're new to the base, you might not have heard of the gay pride parade. It's going to be held in town next Sunday, and we're all allowed to march in it."

"Oh! No, I hadn't heard. Next Sunday? Er… I'll have to check my schedule."

"It'll be great fun. There will be music, and floats, and costumes, and prizes for the best costume. I hope you can make it."

"Yes... well, I'll try to be there. Just have to check my schedule first. I've been more busy than usual these days."

"It's voluntary, of course, sir. But, just between you and me, it would be a good career move. General Coddle frowns upon officers who don't attend."

"Oh, I see. Yes, well...thanks for the advice. And thanks for the device. If anyone asks me, I'll just tell them it's a mice device."

"A mice device. That's a good one, sir."

"I'll have it back to you in the morning. See you then."

CHAPTER 15

Upon leaving the communications building Cassandra was approached by a young, bespectacled, ponytailed woman dressed in a pant suit.

"Oh, excuse me, officer. Are you Captain Cassandra?"

"Yes, ma'am." He hoped she would not inquire about the "mice device" package he was trying his best to conceal behind his back.

"I'm Cynthia Forrest-Green. I teach fifth-grade here at the base school."

"Nice to meet you. Fifth grade? Sounds like a tough job. I think I'd rather clean out a machine gun nest than face a class of fifth graders."

"Yes, it is a battle, for sure. That's why I wanted to talk with you. I'm trying to recruit some of the male officers to come in to speak to my students – especially during the sex education unit. You know how it is with boys. They're more likely to listen to a man."

She spoke very earnestly. In fact, Cassandra could not remember meeting so many earnest people in such a short space of time as he had at Fort Camp. Nevertheless, he was reluctant to get pulled in. He had no desire to talk with fifth-grade boys about anything – let alone sex education.

"Yep, yep. Boys can be difficult. That's for sure." He nodded and bit his lip. "That's for sure."

"So I was hoping you might be willing to volunteer an hour to come in and talk with the class someday," Cynthia said expectantly, "perhaps share your own experience."

"Share my experience? Uh, well, I don't know..."

"Oh, what I really mean is to share your knowledge."

"Uh, I see. Well, uh, what do they teach in sex education these days?"

"Oh, nothing controversial – just the basics: same-sex marriage, contraceptive techniques, abortion, sterilization. Just the basics."

"Sterilization? Why do fifth graders need to know about sterilization?"

"To save the planet from overpopulation, Captain: to save the rainforest and the polar bears. Don't you think it's important to save the planet for the next generation?"

Her earnestness was an argument in itself.

"Well, sure. But if everyone gets sterilized there's not going to be any next generation. Who's going to appreciate the rainforest then? The polar bears?"

"Well, naturally, some people will be allowed to breed. They would have to be government-approved, of course."

"Umm... I don't know. Sounds kind of intrusive to me. What do the Muslim parents think about all this?"

"All the Muslim children are exempt from the sex education unit. We try to be sensitive to other cultural traditions."

"Well, how about the Army's cultural traditions? Our tradition is to defend the country. And you have to have boots on the ground to do that. If everybody opts out of parenthood who's going to fight our wars?"

"We're teaching our students to create a world without war."

"You are? How do you do that?" he asked skeptically.

"We have a unit on peace studies, Captain." She

seemed confident that this explanation was sufficient to dispel any doubts.

"Well, suppose they aren't teaching peace studies over in Iran? Doesn't that put us at a disadvantage?"

"Not at all. Once the people of Iran see that we mean them no harm, they won't feel the need to be defensive. You have to give peace a chance, Captain."

"Yeah, but I'd like to give it at least a fighting chance. But look," he said, producing the package, "I'm in a rush right now. I've got to deliver this package. Can I get back to you, Miss… What was the name again?"

"Ms. …Ms. Forrest-Green, but you can call me Cynthia."

"Nice meeting you, Cynthia," he said as he backed away. "Sorry I can't talk right now. I'll be in touch. Bye, now. Bye."

CHAPTER 16

As twilight settled over Fort Camp, the Muslim command center shifted into high gear. Some officers scurried about, others conferred in small groups, still others were studying computer screens. In one corner, Major Osama, Lieutenant Jabar, and another bearded officer, Captain Nasrallah went over a map together. They looked up as Colonel Faisal entered the room.

"Ah! Colonel. Were you able to find what you were looking for?"

"Yes, I have the information I need. And if anyone wants to make a joke about my 'little friend,' he'd better think twice. By Allah, I have sacrificed much for the cause, but there is only so much that a man can put up with."

"It won't be long now, Colonel."

"By Allah, once we have triumphed, I will strangle him with my own hands."

Major Osama, who had studied sharia law in his youth, was shocked.

"But no, Colonel! That is forbidden. According to law he must be thrown off a high building."

"It is also permitted to crush such a one with stones," added Captain Nasrallah helpfully.

"You could throw him off a building, and *then* crush

him with stones," offered Lieutenant Jabar.

"All right, all right, enough!" said Faisal, restraining his anger. "Let's get down to business. Major Osama, let's have that report."

Meanwhile, under cover of a darkening sky, Captain Cassandra was busy attaching the transmitter portion of the listening device to the outside wall of the command center. That done, he scurried to the shadow of a nearby building and put on the headphones. He immediately began to pick up the conversation inside.

"... So, very shortly, Operation Crescent Moon becomes operational. Any questions? Captain Nasrallah?"

"How will we know the precise time to make our move?"

"We will get the go signal from our man in the Pentagon," replied Major Osama.

Lieutenant Jabar was incredulous.

"We have a man in the Pentagon?"

Major Osama allowed himself a slight smile.

"In the Pentagon, in Homeland Security, in the FBI, even in the White House."

"By Allah!" exulted Jabar.

All the officers were now seated facing toward one side of the room. At the front, Major Osama stood behind a table that was spread with papers and charts. It was his job to lay out the essentials of the plan and to answer questions.

"How about the other services? The Navy?" asked Nasrallah.

"I wouldn't worry about the Navy. All the top slots have been filled by homosexuals." Osama said this without a trace of irony or innuendo.

Captain Nasrallah, however, could not let the occasion pass.

"You mean all the rear admirals have been replaced

by – ”

“Exactly,” said Osama, cutting him off. He was not sure whether it was proper to joke about sinful activity.

“The rear admirals…?” Lieutenant Jabar was confused at first. Then it struck him. “I get it. All the rear admirals have been replaced by queer admirals! By Allah, that is funny!”

Some of the others stared at him disapprovingly.

Jabar shrugged his shoulders.

“Why don’t we just kill all the gays now?”

“That would be premature eradication, Lieutenant,” explained Nasrallah. “For now, they serve our purpose. It’s simple. The more gays, the less straights. Enlistments drop – and we volunteer to fill the quotas. You see?”

“That is awesome!”

“So for now we leave the gays in peace. Afterwards is a different story. When we take over, we will appoint a vice admiral to deal with the queer admirals.”

“A vice admiral! By Allah!” Lieutenant Jabar began to laugh excessively, but stifled himself when he saw that the others were staring at him.

CHAPTER 17

When Captain Cassandra had attached the transmitter to the wall of the command center he had inadvertently trapped a bee inside the suction cup which held the device to the wall. This hadn't been a problem for the first few minutes, as the bee had simply contented itself with exploring the inside of the transmitter cup. Then it started to buzz angrily and the sound of voices in Cassandra's headphones suddenly mingled with what sounded like a barber's clipper at close range. Cassandra was momentarily startled and confused. Snatches of conversation alternated with the buzzing sound and he was only able to pick up bits and pieces of the conversation. This went on for almost two minutes, then, mercifully, it abruptly stopped as the bee paused to reassess the situation.

Inside, Major Osama was wrapping up his part of the meeting.

"... So, if there are no more questions, let me turn the briefing over to Colonel Faisal."

Colonel Faisal stood up, picked up a wooden pointer, and pointed to a large wall map that just happened to be located about 12 inches distant from the transmitter on the outside wall.

"Thank you, Major. All right, here's how things stand.

Our teams are poised to take control of Fort Cable, Ft. Garland, Fort Rainbow, and Camp Carter. Fort Blister, for all intents and purposes, is already ours. You know the plans for the takeover here. General Coddle will soon experience a different kind of cultural exchange. Meanwhile, our mobile units will secure these communication centers – *HERE*! *HERE*! and *HERE*!"

With each "Here!" he whacked the map with the heavy wooden pointer, and each time Cassandra winced and put up his hands to his headphones.

"Then our special ops teams will take control of the main bridges to Washington – *HERE*! *HERE*! and *HERE*!"

Again, he whacked the map three times, and again Cassandra felt the pain. At the same time the bee resumed its buzzing. The combined effect caused Cassandra to jump up, snatch the headphones from his ears, and toss them to the ground. In his agitation he managed to knock over some empty crates he had been hiding behind.

Colonel Faisal detected the noise but continued as though nothing had happened.

"We think the president will quickly realize the hopelessness of the situation, and will be willing to come to terms. So that's it for now. Major Osama and Captain Nasrallah will fill you in on the details." Then he turned to an officer standing nearby and spoke in a lower voice. "Sergeant Akbar, check outside. I thought I heard something."

Outside, Captain Cassandra spotted Sergeant Akbar coming out the door some sixty feet away. He grabbed the headphones and beat a hasty retreat through the darkness in the direction of his quarters.

CHAPTER 18

His heart pumping rapidly, Cassandra entered his quarters, still clutching the headphones. He closed the door quickly, pressed up against it, and listened intently. Hearing nothing, he let out his breath, wiped his brow and put down what was left of the mice device. Cassandra needed a drink, but first he needed to make a call. He walked away from the door, took out his cell phone, and punched in a number.

"Hi, Larry, it's Jim. Say, can you talk freely?"

"Sure, nobody here but my shadow."

"Good. Listen, there's something going on here that worries me: something ominous – maybe some kind of coup in the making. Now, I tried to bring it up with Coddle, but I can't get through to him. Seems to think he's running some kind of multicultural exchange club. Look, Larry, I think this thing – whatever it is – is going down soon. There's no time for me to go through proper channels. You have good contacts. Do you know anyone who's higher up that I can confide in? I mean, someone who will listen to the evidence. And it's got to be someone who's not afraid to take action."

"Whoa! Slow down! This is pretty heavy stuff. You're going to get yourself in trouble if you're not careful. Don't forget "coup" rhymes with "cuckoo." You can't go around making accusations like that without solid evidence. What kind of evidence do you have?"

"I can't go into details. You'll just have to take my word for it. Look, you know I don't shoot from the hip."

"Okay. I still think you're playing with dynamite, but if you have to see someone, it would be Jack Panzer."

"General Jack Panzer? Yes, I've heard the name. He's at the Pentagon, isn't he?"

"When he's not hunting down bad guys."

"Listen, do you think you can make arrangements for me to meet him?"

"Yeah, I should be able to work something out."

"Good. Get back to me as soon as you know."

"You got it, Jim. But like I say, it's your funeral."

"Thanks, Larry, I'll be waiting for your call."

Cassandra went to the fridge, took out a can of beer, and slumped onto the couch. He began to wonder if he had been too hasty. Was it as bad as he thought? Or was he jumping to unwarranted conclusions? Maybe the talk of capturing communications centers and bridges that he had overheard was merely part of some war games exercise that he wasn't privy to. Was he adding two and two and coming up with twenty-two? He realized he would look like a fool if his suspicions were unfounded. Go to the Pentagon and what then? Be laughed at? Or worse, he could find himself under investigation.

He had heard of people being demoted or even discharged on charges of Islamophobia. These days the Army didn't take kindly to even a hint of cultural insensitivity. Maybe he should have waited before calling Larry – given himself a chance to calm down, collect his thoughts. And how well did he really know Larry, after all? They had been friends once, but he hadn't seen Larry in years. People change over time, he knew, and sometimes they change radically. He had seen easy-going acquaintances change into paranoid conspiracy—

nuts, and he had known atheists who were now pious church-goers. More to the point, he knew there had been several cases of soldiers converting to Islam and turning jihadist. Could Larry be trusted?

He realized he was working himself up and would soon reach a point where these ruminations would take on a life of their own, circling around in his head for the next three hours and leaving him mentally exhausted. Determined to dismiss his doubts before they got the best of him, he took a sip of beer and clicked on the TV.

A newscast was in progress. The two anchors, an attractive blonde and a neatly-groomed man, seemed very sincere but at the same time somewhat clueless concerning the significance of the events which they reported. Despite the gravity of the news, their presentation was consistently upbeat.

'More earnestness,' thought Cassandra. 'Doesn't matter what kind of nonsense they talk, as long as it's all in earnest.'

"Welcome back, everyone; it's the bottom of the hour. And here are the stories that are making news. A new study reveals a mysterious drop-off in military enlistments over the past year. The study, conducted by the National Bureau of Compliance, reveals a thirty-five percent drop in enlistments, and a forty percent drop in re-enlistments.

Experts are baffled by the decline, and are searching for clues to explain the recruitment gap. When asked what the Army plans to do about the problem, Army Chief of Recruitment, General Armani Versace, said that the Army is exploring the possibility of designing more stylish uniforms as an incentive to today's fashion-conscious young men and women."

At this point she turned to her co-host.

"I don't know, Emerson, it sounds like a serious problem. What do you make of it?"

"Casey, that's a tough one to figure, especially when you consider that the military has become much more accommodating of different lifestyles. Let's hope that the new uniforms do the trick."

He turned to face the camera.

"In other news, the U.S. has pulled its last remaining troops out of the Islamic Republic of Afghanistan. White House Press Secretary Richie Leeks explained that there is no further need for a U.S. presence now that democracy has been firmly established. To mark the occasion, Afghanis celebrated their newfound freedom with the execution of twelve apostates in Kabul's Taliban Square. The apostates were all recent converts to Christianity… Hmmm, twelve apostates. There seems to be some significance there, but I'm not sure what it is. Any ideas, Casey?"

"No," said Casey, who was also at a loss. "Muslims often celebrate their cultural values on the eleventh day of the month, but as far as I know there's no significance to the number twelve. Well, in other news, a United States Navy Destroyer, The USS Diversity, has been captured by pirates off the coast of Somalia. When asked why the destroyer's crew had been unable to stop the hijacking, Rear Admiral Constance Kilroy explained that the Navy's rules of engagement prohibit servicemen from firing on teenagers. Since the crew were unable to distinguish which of the pirates were underage, the Captain was required under Navy regulations to surrender the ship. The leader of the pirates is now demanding a ransom of 30 million dollars for the return of the ship and crew. The pirates have further stipulated that the ransom be paid either in gold or in Chinese Yuan, rather than in U.S. Dollars. Emerson?"

"Meanwhile, in Washington the president and his security advisors will meet tomorrow to discuss these and other developments – "

Cassandra switched to the movie channel. The wartime classic, *Casablanca*, was playing. It was the scene where Rick and Sam are alone in the darkened café and the disconsolate Rick utters the famous line about pre-war American complacency:

"I bet they're asleep in New York. I bet they're asleep all over America."

"I bet they're asleep in Washington, too," thought Cassandra. But before too many more minutes had passed, he too was nodding asleep and the soothing words from the screen merged seamlessly with his dreamy imaginings.

CHAPTER 19

The security meetings in the White House Situation Room rarely started on time. And today was no exception. As usual, it was the president who held things up. Although President Prince was keen about issues such as gay rights and the minimum wage, national security was not high on his list of priorities. However, since new threats to American security were emerging on an almost daily basis, security briefings could not be altogether avoided. Twenty minutes after the scheduled start time, President Prince convened the meeting.

"Secretary Apoligeto, why don't you bring us up to date on Homeland Security?" He was addressing Jennifer Apoligeto, the Secretary of Homeland Security. Although childless, Apoligeto had a matronly appearance and, for that matter, matronly concerns.

"Thank you, Mr. President," she replied. "Since our last meeting, we've completed a thorough revision of the color-coded threat level alert." At this point, she produced a large chart and showed it to the others.

"As you can see on this chart, the current alert uses very bold primary colors such as red and orange. Our psychologists tell us that these colors make many people feel uncomfortable. Red, for example, is unnecessarily alarmist. As a result we have developed a new, nonthreatening threat chart which you can see here." Secretary Apoligeto displayed a second chart.

"As you can see, the new colors are much friendlier. We've replaced red with a subtle shade of pink. And instead of orange we've substituted a warm ochre. And here," she said pointing to the middle of the chart, "we've introduced a soft pastel shade of yellow. We did have trouble deciding on a replacement for the blue, but fortunately my decorator, Emilio, suggested the very lovely shade of lavender you see here – "

This was too much for Senator Tom Hartland, a conservative member of the Armed Services Committee. The combative senator stood up, and interrupting the secretary's discourse on design, he addressed the president.

"With all due respect, Mr. President, this isn't the home decorating channel. What are we doing talking about pastels for pansies when we have terrorists bombing our bases and embassies all over the world?"

"Tom, you know you're not supposed to use that word in these meetings," said the president with a hint of reproach.

"Embassies?"

"You know perfectly well that "terrorist" is no longer part of the official lexicon."

"Okay, then. All I'm saying is that we've got to do something to stop these jihad attacks."

"There you go again, Tom."

"Uh, Mr. President, I don't see how we can fight something if we can't name it."

"It's just a matter of using the proper, non-offensive terminology. I think what you are referring to are 'man-caused tragedies'." This was in reference to a phrase coined by Secretary Apoligeto to describe terrorist attacks. The president glanced at her and she nodded in affirmation. He continued:

"Naturally, I'm just as concerned as you are about

these distressing events. But I think we have to stay focused on the really important issues. Uh...General Johnson, do you have that report ready?"

General Johnson, a hearty, broad-shouldered man who looked young for a general, stood up and displayed a report.

"Yes, sir. I have the results of a new study conducted by our LGBTU research unit, and I'm afraid we're still not up to snuff. We're not quite meeting the quotas we established for LGBTU soldiers, sailors, and airpersons –"

The president interrupted. "I'm afraid I don't recall what the 'U' stands for."

"That's 'undecided,' sir. Anyway, we're only at 28 percent and we were hoping by this time it would be closer to 33 percent."

"Well, we've got to do better than that. Do you think you can throw more resources into the new recruitment campaign?"

"I'll do my best."

Unable to restrain himself any longer, Senator Hartland rose again. He spoke heatedly:

"If I may speak my mind, Mr. President, this is only throwing fuel on the fire. While we're pussy footing around with these diversity quotas, our enemies are building their militaries faster than McDonald's makes burgers. The current strength level of the Chinese army is twelve million, the North Koreans have seven million, the Turks have five million, and the Islamic Republic of Iran has four million. Not to mention the Islamic Republic of Egypt, the Islamic Republic of Yemen, and the Islamic Republic of Pakistan. Even the damn Venezuelan army can field 800,000 men. And we're down to 500,000 and falling. Now, if you'll permit me to say so, everybody here knows damn well why that is. It's because no normal kid wants to serve in an army that's run...like a damn queer bathhouse!"

This last remark brought Senator Franky Barnstable to his feet. He was a liberal member of the Armed Services Committee and, despite his burly look, he spoke with a pronounced lisp.

"Mitha Pwesident, Mitha Pwesident, this man is a bigot and a wacist! I wequest that he be wemoved from this chamber at once!"

"Thank you, Senator Barnstable," said the president. Frowning, he turned on Hartland.

"Senator Hartland, I find your language deeply offensive, and I'm sure everybody else here feels the same way. I suggest you find some other way to express your sentiments."

"All I'm saying is that our Army is leaking troops like a sieve, and we've got to find some way to plug the dike!"

The president was thoroughly exasperated. "Plug the dyke? Senator, I think we've heard just about enough from you. My administration has fought hard for equality in the Armed Services, and we're not going back on that commitment. As my predecessor said, 'No American should be denied the right to serve the country he loves, because of who he loves.'"

When he spoke in this manner, he had a habit of thrusting his prominent jaw upward and pressing his lips together, making him look like Benito Mussolini reincarnated in a thinner, trimmer form. Regaining his composure, he continued in a more conciliatory fashion. "Er…besides, General Johnson assures me that he has a plan for raising troop levels. General Johnson, could you expand on that?"

"Certainly, Mr. President," said the general. "But before I do, let me say that I share your sense of outrage at the Senator's attitude. As you know, we're trying to build a new type of army – an army that's based on tolerance, and openness, and – as you put it so well – on love. Now there may be a few people out there who won't join up because they are intolerant of differences. Well, frankly, we think these are the kind of people that don't belong in the army in the first place."

Senator Hartland rolled his eyes, but kept silent. General Johnson continued:

"Now, as the president says, we are working on a new plan to bring the military back up to strength. The plan is to allow illeg...I mean undocumented residents to serve in the military alongside U.S. troops. We know there are hundreds of thousands now living in this country who would jump at the chance."

"Are you sure that's a good idea, General? It sounds like a drastic step."

"I know what you're thinking, sir. But our top people have worked out the details and it looks like a win-win situation. The army's a tough life and, frankly, a lot of our citizens have grown soft. These immigrants will take the jobs that no one else wants to do."

The president considered. "Hmm. How do you think the public will react?"

General Johnson punched the air for emphasis. "They'll love it, Mr. President. This is a plan that will save the taxpayer a load of money. You see, we figure these illegals will be willing to accept a lower pay scale than your average American soldier. As compensation we put 'em on the fast track to citizenship. And you know what that means, Mr. President. They'll be voting in no time."

"Well, when you put it that way, it does seem to make sense. I think that's a plan I can go along with.... Now, I know some of you want to leave early today to attend the rally on the Mall in support of the new Islamic center there. My core team will remain here with me to discuss some other matters. Thank you for coming."

Most of those present in the room got up to leave. Several of them were heavily bearded men of a Middle-Eastern appearance. They had kept silent during the meeting but they had followed the discussion with great interest. The satisfied looks on their faces suggested that they were pleased with the direction it had taken.

CHAPTER 20

Cassandra had heard about the indignities visited on passengers passing through airport security but, being an officer, had up until now been spared the stop-and-frisk routine. Today, however, was different. For some reason, he had been shunted into the regular passenger line and was now facing a burly Muslim TSA agent. He assumed the man was Muslim because of his beard and the skull cap he wore.

The TSA agent proceeded to pat down Cassandra in a rather rough manner.

"Hey! Take it easy! Can't you see I'm an officer?"

"Everyone gets treated the same here, mister."

Meanwhile, in the next aisle, a female TSA agent wearing a hijab was waving through two women dressed in head-to-toe burqas. No attempt was made to search them.

"Good morning, sisters. Have a nice flight," said the agent warmly.

The big TSA agent paused from his frisking activities and smiled broadly at the burqa-clad women as they continued on.

"Assalamu alaykum, sisters."

The burqa-clad women nodded and passed by.

"Can I go now?" asked Cassandra impatiently. "I'm

late for my flight."

"Not so fast! Open your mouth."

"Open my mouth?"

"You heard what I said."

Cassandra reluctantly opened his mouth. The TSA officer shined a flashlight inside.

"Say aaah."

"Aaah."

"Okay, you can go."

Somewhat shaken and astonished by his experience, Cassandra gathered his belongings and headed toward the gate.

CHAPTER 21

Making his way down the aisle of the plane, Cassandra passed a group of six imams in robes and prayer caps seated together in two rows, one behind the other. This unnerved him but he determined not to jump to conclusions. After all, the chances that they would pose any threat were at least a million to one. They had probably just attended a religious conference and were on their way home.

One of the imams gave Cassandra a piercing look and another smiled in what Cassandra was sure was a contemptuous manner. By sheer coincidence, two of the seats in the row directly behind the imams were occupied by two nuns. They wore black habits and white wimples, and they smiled sweetly at Cassandra.

Cassandra took the aisle seat that was assigned to him. It was two rows behind the nuns and it placed him opposite a mother and her daughter, a girl of six or seven. He picked up a flight magazine from the seat pocket in front, and relaxed back in his own seat. One of the articles was on airline safety and how much it had improved over the years. This caught his interest and he began to read. According to the article's author, the chances of an accident for any particular flight were, just as Cassandra had guessed, about a million to one.

He had nearly forgotten the imams when, a few moments later, he heard a murmuring sound coming from some rows ahead. He lowered the magazine and looked over the top. The sound was unmistakable now. The imams were praying in Arabic. One was leading and the others responding.

The plane was still at the gate awaiting instructions, but the doors had been closed, cutting off any hope of escape. Cassandra quickly recalculated the odds. What had seemed a million to one probability suddenly dropped to the vicinity of a hundred to one. And even that might be optimistic, he thought. The other passengers were obviously thinking the same thing. The looks on the faces of those nearby mirrored the anxiety he was feeling.

The praying continued at a higher volume, punctuated at intervals with shouts of "Allahu akbar." In the row behind the imams, the nuns had begun to quietly pray the rosary. Other passengers exchanged worried glances. Still, no one made a move to do anything about it. There were certain unwritten rules in American society that everyone recognized and abided by. And one of them was that it was better to risk death than be thought a bigot.

Finally, Cassandra signaled to a flight attendant who was coming down the aisle from the back of the plane. He whispered to her and pointed in the direction of the imams.

The flight attendant seemed to grasp the situation. She nodded to Cassandra and walked toward the front of the plane, glancing in the direction of the imams as she passed by. Continuing down the aisle, she knocked on the cockpit door and entered.

Inside the cockpit, she leaned over the pilot and whispered in his ear. He nodded in affirmation and picked up a mic.

"Security, we have a problem..."

"Allahu Akbar!" Back in the cabin, the imams were praying more loudly and more fervently. The nuns were praying more intensely too, their fingers firmly squeezing each bead. The passengers in the rear of the plane knew something was amiss but couldn't make out what was wrong. Those closer to the scene, however, gripped their arm rests and threw panicky glances at one another. Across the aisle from Cassandra, the frightened child turned to her mother.

"Mommy, I'm scared," she sobbed.

At that instant, the flight attendant opened a door near the front of the plane, and several plainclothes security agents burst in. They moved quickly in the direction of the imams but, to everyone's astonishment, they passed by the clerics and stopped at the nuns' row. The nuns, who were still fingering their rosaries, looked up in surprise.

"Okay, sisters, you'd better hand those over and come with us," said the lead agent. From the tone of his voice, it was clear that he expected immediate compliance.

"But I...I don't understand," said the nun who was closest to the aisle.

The agent was impatient. "You'll have plenty of time to explain later, sister. Right now you need to come with us."

As the agents accompanied the startled nuns to the plane's exit, the other passengers looked on in disbelief. Cassandra was surprised as well, but not as much as he would have been a week earlier. He was becoming accustomed to the unexpected. Besides, he reasoned, whatever ordeal the two sisters now faced, they were at least lucky to be off the "Hindenburg" – as he now thought of the doomed plane.

The imams, however, had stopped praying. Their faces beamed with smug satisfaction. Apparently, their prayers had been answered. The two representatives of the rival faith had been banished from their presence.

"Allahu Akbar." The words meant "Allah is greater." And, for the moment at least, the imams seemed to have proved the point.

Although the praying had ceased, the atmosphere of panic it had created remained a palpable presence in the cabin. Many of the traumatized passengers were still in shock. They continued to grip their seat rests or the hands of their loved ones. In the seat across from Cassandra's, the worried mother tried to comfort her sobbing child.

The crew, however, had retained its composure. As the ramp was retracted from the door of the jetliner, the flight attendant's upbeat voice could be heard over the intercom.

"We apologize for the delay in getting started. We are now ready for departure. Please make sure your seat belts are fastened and your trays locked in their upright position. Thank you for flying our friendly skies. Enjoy your flight!"

Cassandra strongly doubted that any of the passengers – with the possible exception of the six robed figures in aisles seven and eight – would enjoy the flight.

CHAPTER 22

At the request of the president, General Johnson had remained behind after the other members of the core team had departed.

"Now that the others have left," said the president, "I'd like to go over the situation in West Tajikistan."

"Well, sir," replied General Johnson, "we've got good evidence that they've crossed the red line you set and are using chemical weapons against their own people."

"I thought that was a pink line?"

"No, sir, you set the pink line for East Tajikistan."

"Hmm. Well, what should we do?"

"I don't think we have any choice but to send them another warning."

"Is that really necessary?"

"I think so, sir. The public will expect something."

"Alright. But this time we should use stronger language. Tell them we are utterly dismayed at the loss of human lives, and...uh...let's see."

"Deeply disturbed?"

"Yes, 'deeply disturbed about the threat to regional stability,' and let's say something about this being 'an unacceptable breach of international accords'."

"Anything else?"

"Yes, tell them we are considering all options...um,

no…better not say that. Just have my secretary work up something and I'll look it over later."

"Yes, sir."

"By the way, who is in charge of our own chemical arsenal?"

"Most of our domestic supply is housed at Fort Camp, sir. It's under the control of … let's see…" General Johnson searched through his smart phone. "Oh, yes, General Coddle. Nothing to worry about there, Mr. President. I hear he keeps a firm hand on the controls."

CHAPTER 23

At that very moment, the hands of General Coddle were busily engaged with manicurist tools. He carefully filed the nails on one hand and held them up for inspection, humming the tune to "Imagine" as he did so. As he was about to tackle the other hand, a knock came at the open door and Lieutenant Lopez entered.

"You wanted to see me, sir?"

"Yes, my boy. I see the annual report on safety procedures for our chemical weapons is due. Who's in charge of the chemical depot these days?"

"You put Colonel Faisal in charge six months ago."

"Oh, yes, Faisal. Good man, good man. Well, ask him if he could fill out these forms when he has a chance."

Coddle handed over some forms.

"Yes, sir."

"Oh! And wish him a happy Ramadan for me," he said cheerily.

CHAPTER 24

The "Hindenburg" arrived safely at Reagan National Airport without further incident. Captain Cassandra, carrying a small travel bag, hurriedly stepped off an escalator, glanced at a time display, and moved briskly toward the airport exit. His cell phone rang and he answered it on the move.

"Hello?... Yes, this is he."

The voice on the other end was that of General Panzer's aide.

"Captain, there's been a change of plans, and your meeting with General Panzer has been postponed until three."

Cassandra stopped short. "Three! But I have to see him right away!"

"I'm afraid it will have to wait, sir. The General's involved with issues of national security."

"But this *is* an issue of national security!" said Cassandra urgently.

"Sorry, there's nothing I can do. Why don't you see some of the sights in the meantime? There's Arlington Cemetery – "

"The whole blasted Army's going to end up in Arlington Cemetery if I don't speak to General Panzer soon!"

"Sorry, sir, it'll have to be three, or not at all."

"All right, all right. Three o'clock. Goodbye." He lowered the phone. "Damn!"

He glanced at a nearby time display. It was 10:25. The clock was ticking and he alone had the information to foil the plot.

CHAPTER 25

Once outside, Cassandra headed for a taxi stand. In the line ahead of him a blind man with a guide dog was waiting his turn. When the next cab arrived, the man and his dog approached it, but to Cassandra's surprise they were shooed away by the cabbie.

"No, no...no! No dogs allowed!" said the cabbie in a Pakistani accent. "Unclean. It is forbidden! Shoo! Shoo, bad dog. Sir, I am sorry, but you must wait for a dhimmi driver."

The blind man, apparently used to this sort of discrimination, shrugged and shuffled over to one side. The cabbie then beckoned to Cassandra.

"You're next, sir. Sorry for the disturbance." He added apologetically, "You understand, it is against our tradition. Please get in."

Cassandra felt somewhat guilty, but he was in no mood to stage a civil rights protest. He had had enough drama for one day. He settled into the back seat.

"Where to?"

"Um, well, I have a few hours to kill. I think I'll do some sightseeing. Why don't you take me to the National Mall?"

The cabbie chuckled good-naturedly.

"Yes, sir! ...Forgive me for my laughter. At first, I thought you said, 'I have a few *houris* to kill.' Kill the hours, Captain, but please don't kill the *houris*. Otherwise, there might not be any left for me."

"The *houris*? Oh yes, the 72 virgins in paradise. Well, I guess that would be a good way to kill a few hours."

"Or a few eternities," added the cabbie.

Before getting into the cab, Cassandra had noticed a discolored bump on the driver's forehead just below the cap. This reminded him of something but he couldn't recall what. Curious, he asked:

"Say, did you hurt yourself? You've got a bump on your head."

"Oh, that is a prayer bump. A practicing Muslim must touch his forehead to the ground in prayer at least thirty-four times a day. So, over time, you develop the bump. That is how you can recognize a truly devout follower of the Prophet. We call it the *zebiba*, Captain."

"The *zebiba*, huh. Say, how do you know I'm a captain?"

"Oh, I drive many officers from the airport," said the driver nonchalantly.

"You know, you look familiar. Have we ever met?"

"I don't think so, Captain," he said guardedly, and then quickly changed the subject. "You will enjoy the Mall. There is a big rally there to support the construction of the new mosque. It will be a very grand mosque. When it is finished you must come back to see it. If you come at night it will be especially beautiful. Imagine with all the lights, and with the crescent moon above. Yes, very beautiful."

Cassandra was surprised to hear the code name.

"The crescent moon? ...Yes, I suppose it will be quite beautiful."

After a few more minutes they came in sight of the Mall.

"We are almost there, Captain," said the cabbie smiling broadly. And then, in words that seemed to carry a double intention: "Yes, we are very close now."

CHAPTER 26

Rallies for and against the proposed Islamic Center were in progress on the Mall. As Captain Cassandra wandered through the crowd, he noticed that a surprising number of the people he passed had the telltale bump on their foreheads. Those with the bumps cast ominous looks in his direction.

Attracted by a sound of shouting nearby he came upon a crowd listening to a fire-breathing imam. Individuals in the crowd carried signs with slogans such as "AMERICA IS THE CANCER, ISLAM IS THE ANSWER," "ISLAM WILL RULE THE WORLD," and "SLAY THOSE WHO INSULT ISLAM." The imam was wild-eyed, robed, and bearded, and he gesticulated wildly as he talked.

“And who is the bitterest enemy of Allah?” he cried out.

“The Jews!” roared the crowd in enthusiastic response.

“And what did Allah do to the disobedient Jews?”

“He made them into pigs and apes!” came the response.

“Muslims! The Christians have a saying: ‘What would Jesus do?’ But we do not ask, ‘What would Jesus do?’ We ask, ‘What would Muhammad do?’ And what did

Muhammad do to the Jews of Quarayza?"

"He cut off their heads!" shouted the crowd.

The imam was growing more agitated. "Yes, all seven hundred of them! And are we not to follow the example of the Prophet? The Prophet said 'the Hour of Resurrection will not come until the Muslims fight the Jews, and the rock and the tree will say 'O Muslim! There is a Jew hiding behind me, come and kill him!'"

Speaking more rapidly now, the imam continued his rant.

"O, Muslims! There are Jews behind every conspiracy and treachery in the world! What shall we do? What would Muhammad do? Oh, Jews, you will pay, your 9/11 is on its way!"

The crowd took up the chant.

"Oh, Jews, you will pay! Your 9/11 is on its way! Oh, Jews, you will pay! Your 9/11 is on its way!"

Cassandra spotted a policeman at the edge of the crowd who was listening to the sermon, and went up to him.

"Excuse me, officer, shouldn't you arrest that man? I mean, it sounds like he's inciting them to violence."

The policeman, who was about ten years older than Cassandra, responded gruffly.

"What's the matter with you? Never heard of freedom of speech? You must have been stationed too long in Libya or someplace. Over here, a man's got the right to speak his mind."

The officer continued in a confiding tone.

"Besides, those are just figures of speech. Arabs use a lot of exaggeration in their language. It's part of their culture... Eh, what's that?"

A middle-aged woman wearing a hijab tugged at the cop's sleeve. She didn't say anything but insistently beckoned him to come with her. Deferring to her insistence he shrugged his shoulder and followed her lead. Cassandra tagged along.

She led them to another, smaller crowd about two hundred feet away and pointed an accusing finger in their direction. Judging by a logo-like banner held up by two of the group members, the rally was hosted by an organization called "Stop Islamization Now." The acronym for that is "SIN," mused Cassandra, but there was nothing about their behavior to suggest vice or recklessness. In comparison to the imam's followers, this group was the soul of restraint. Even the signs they carried bespoke a certain self-discipline: "NO CALIPHATE STATE," "MOSQUE-FREE ZONE," NO MINARETS ON OUR MALL."

The speaker addressing them was a mild-looking, clean-shaven, bespectacled man in his fifties. Cassandra thought he was making a reasonable case.

"Let's be sure that we all understand that we have nothing against Muslims. Muslims are our neighbors. But we should be worried about sharia law. Because once sharia law takes hold, you can say goodbye to our Constitution. You won't have freedom of speech any more, or freedom of religion. Women will be denied their rights, and Jews will be persecuted – "

A man in the crowd interrupted. "But didn't the Muslims protect the Jews under their rule?"

"Sometimes they did, but not always. Unfortunately, Islam has a long record of anti-Semitism, starting with Muhammad, himself, who once ordered the beheading of 700 men of the Jews of Quarayza. In the Koran, Jews are often referred to as 'apes' and 'pigs' – "

"Okay, you, that's enough," barked the police officer indignantly. And with that, he went up to the front and grabbed the speaker by the arm.

"I guess I know hate speech when I hear it. You're under arrest for defamation of a prophet."

"But officer," protested the speaker, "I was just quoting from the Koran..."

"Tell it to the judge, mister."

CHAPTER 27

On any other day, Cassandra might have tried to intervene. He had a strong sense of fairness and he was sure the officer had acted unjustly. On the other hand, he reflected, others in the SIN group were trying to reason with the cop. They would also know lawyers to contact, and would be able to come up with bail for their speaker if any was needed.

Moreover, Cassandra had a mission of his own. He had his own, one-man stop-Islamization project to attend to and he couldn't allow himself to be deterred from it – couldn't afford to risk the possibility of spending the afternoon in a precinct station as a witness to a hate crime. He imagined himself as a movie hero in a spy thriller who had only hours left to deliver the code that would save the nation from disaster. Such a man would not allow himself to be distracted by obtuse law enforcement agents or by seductive brunettes planted in his hotel room by enemy operatives.

Then again, what movie hero would permit himself to waste two hours of the precious time allotted to him in wandering around the National Mall while the fate of the nation lay in the balance?

Cassandra decided he was no hero. He had no back up strategy to deal with the sudden change of plans, and he could think of nothing else to do with himself except to pass his time among the tourists until his appointed rendezvous with General Panzer.

He moved on in the direction of the Washington Monument and came upon another crowd of protesters. They were demonstrating in favor of the mosque but, curiously, there didn't seem to be any Muslims among them. Judging from the banners and posters they displayed, these people were leftists and feminists of the more radical variety. The large banners announced their various group affiliations: "COMMUNIST PARTY USA," "COMMUNIST YOUTH LEAGUE," "SOCIALIST WORKERS UNITED," "FEMINISTS FOR ISLAM," and "CHRISTIANS UNITED FOR PEACE AND LOVE."

Some of the demonstrators carried individual signs with slogans such as: "KEEP YOUR BAN OFF MY BURQA," "THE PEOPLE'S MALL," "EQUAL PRAY IS JUST FAIR PLAY," and "LAY OFF ISLAM, UNCLE SAM!" Unlike the hand-painted signs displayed at the SIN gathering, these signs looked like they were run off a printing press. America's leftists, thought Cassandra, were a boon to the sign-making industry. The only hand-printed sign was carried by a girl named Maria. Cassandra assumed that must be her name, for the sign read, "MY NAME IS MARIA AND I'M FOR SHARIA."

"I just met a girl named Sharia," thought Cassandra. He thought this so clever that he tried to mentally construct more new lyrics for the old standard. He was hit by a sudden inspiration. "How about this?" he said to himself:

"Sharia! Say it soft and it's almost like slaying. Say it loud and they'll kill you for straying."

This pleased him so much that he said it over in his head several times. Before he could come up with any more lyrics, however, his concentration was broken by a nearby group of protesters who had taken up a chant of "Hey! Hey! U.S.A! How many Turks did you kill today?"

His hopes for creating a new Broadway classic were further interrupted by the approach of a young woman with long dark hair who was dressed in jeans and a red T-shirt emblazoned with the words "Anarchists for Islam." Despite the frown on her face, she was fairly good-looking. This, thought Cassandra, might just be the amorous brunette who had been sent to seduce him.

The young anarchist handed a pamphlet to Cassandra

"Whose side are you on, soldier?" she demanded.

"Oh, I don't know. What's the choice?" asked Cassandra.

"Are you for the mosque or against it?"

Near her was a large poster depicting the gigantic proposed mosque. Cassandra pointed to it.

"Is that it? Well, it sort of blocks the view, doesn't it? I mean, where's the Washington Monument?"

"The Washington Monument is a symbol of the white male phallocentric power establishment. It is offensive to women and to people of color. However, as a gesture of conciliation, the Mosque Planning Commission has agreed to keep it. It will serve as the minaret to the grand mosque."

Her tone was entirely humorless. Next to her, thought Cassandra, Cynthia Forrest-Green was a sparkling conversationalist.

"But won't it still be a white power structure?" he countered.

"No, it will be reduced in height by two hundred feet to make it conform to the proportions of the mosque. Then it will be bathed in a perpetual green light."

"Green light, huh? Well, whoever gave the green light to this project ought to have his head examined. I... what the..."

At that instant he was pushed aside by a reporter and a TV camera crew. The TV reporter spoke into a mic and then thrust it in front of the activist.

"Miss, you seem to be one of the leaders here. May I ask you a few questions?"

"Of course."

"Many people say that a mosque doesn't belong on the Mall. What do you say?"

"Many people are intolerant and bigoted. Many people would like to deny freedom of worship to Muslims. We are here to stand in solidarity with the peaceful people of Islam. And we are here to stand against the enemies of freedom!"

"And is there anything else you would like to say to the American people?"

"Yes. The Mall belongs to all the people – not just to the big business interests, not just to the tourist industry, not just to the warmongers who want to build monuments to imperialism!"

At this, she threw an accusing stare at Cassandra, causing others to momentarily turn to look at the uniformed imperialist. Then she continued in an impassioned voice.

"I ask the American people to join us in our fight against oppression and Islamophobia. Don't let this happen in America! Don't let the haters win! Don't take away our right to pray!"

CHAPTER 28

Unknown to Cassandra, the events on the Mall were being watched by a national audience, including several Muslim officers in the command center at Fort Camp. Colonel Faisal, who was among them, clicked off the TV and turned to his companions.

"Filthy atheist dogs! We will deal with them when the time comes."

"By Allah, that will be a glorious day!" exulted Major Osama.

"But you must give them credit," added Faisal. "They are smoothing the path for Allah. Once the coup is underway, our friends on the left will mount massive demonstrations in over twenty cities. That way, it will seem that our takeover has popular support – the will of the people, you know. Of course, it is really the will of Allah."

He turned toward a bank of computers.

"Now, let's do a final systems check."

A young soldier who seemed also to be a computer specialist began to push some switches on a console. After that, he typed in a series of codes on the keyboard in front of him.

"Everything checks out, Colonel. We can take control of the major cable news networks whenever we wish. It's all done remotely."

Colonel Faisal was pleased.

"They won't even know what's happening until it's too late. Their computers will tell them that everything is running normally. It's a brilliant technology. The Jews invented it, of course."

Major Osama was shocked.

"But Colonel, is it right to use Jewish technology? I mean – "

He was interrupted by the Colonel's soothing reassurance.

"Life is a chess game that Allah plays. If he chooses to use some Jewish pawns, who are we to question his will?"

CHAPTER 29

The spacious waiting room outside General Panzer's Pentagon office was paneled in oak. Around the room hung large paintings of military heroes from different eras. Cassandra recognized several of them – Patton, MacArthur, Lee – but he wasn't sure about some of the others.

He was greeted by General Panzer's aide, a young officer who, unlike the personnel at Fort Camp, was dressed in full uniform.

"The General will see you in just a few minutes, sir. Have a seat."

"Thank you. I might just look around, if you don't mind"

"Go right ahead, sir."

Cassandra inspected one of the largest paintings – a full-length portrait of a Revolutionary War-era officer. His uniform, however, seemed more elaborate than those worn by American generals of the period.

"Interesting painting. I know I've seen it before, but I can't quite place the face."

"That's Baron von Steuben, sir. He helped General Washington train the troops at Valley Forge. General Panzer says he was a great patriot, even though he was a German."

"Well, I guess that means General Panzer must be a bit of a patriot too."

"He definitely is."

The phone on his desk buzzed and he picked it up.

"Yes sir, he's here."

He looked up at Cassandra.

"The General will see you now, Captain."

CHAPTER 30

The aide opened the door to a larger oak-lined office and Cassandra was ushered into the formidable presence of General Jack Panzer. Panzer was in his early fifties, tall, broad-shouldered, and ruggedly handsome – with the emphasis on "ruggedly." The look of self-assurance on his square-jawed face was matched by the confident tone in which he spoke.

"Come in, Captain. Take a seat."

Cassandra saluted smartly. "Thank you, sir."

"Cigar, Captain?"

"Oh, no thanks."

"Mind if I indulge?"

"Not at all, sir."

Panzer removed a cigar from a box, cut off the tip with a large guillotine-type cutter that sat on his desk, and lit it. He took a casual puff before addressing Cassandra again.

"I understand you're from Fort Camp, Captain."

"Yes, sir."

"How's the discipline there? A bit lax?"

"Well, to be honest, the place could use a little straightening up."

"That doesn't surprise me. General Coddle and I were classmates at West Point. We used to call him

'Mollycoddle'."

Cassandra chuckled appreciatively.

"'Mollycoddle'. Yes, well, that does seem to fit."

"Glad to see you have a sense of humor, Captain, but I know you didn't come here to engage in small talk. What's on your mind?"

"Well, General, I suppose it has to do with the lack of discipline you mentioned – lack of oversight, really. Something pretty drastic seems to be happening and no one's paying attention. What I mean is... well, I, I..."

"Let's have it straight, Captain. You can level with me."

"Well, General, I... well, have you ever noticed that in recent months a large number of Muslim officers have been moving into positions of authority?"

"As a matter of fact, Captain, I have. I pride myself on keeping up with changes that others miss."

"Well, then, sir, I'll come right to the point. General, this may sound incredible, but I think I've got good evidence of a plot to take over the military, and I think it's going to happen very soon."

"I know about the plot, Captain."

Cassandra was both surprised and relieved.

"You know about it, too? Thank God. I was afraid you wouldn't believe me. General, you don't know what a relief this is."

He hesitated.

"Can you tell me how you plan to stop them? Can you nip it in the bud? I mean, there isn't much time..."

"On the contrary, Captain, time is on our side."

"You mean you'll let it play out a little longer, find out everyone who's involved, then round them up?"

"What I mean, Captain, is that the coup will proceed as planned."

Cassandra was suddenly doubtful.

"I'm afraid I don't follow you, sir."

Panzer blew out a ring of smoke and put down his

cigar.

"Captain, have you ever noticed that the Army's gone weak? Flabby? Badly in need of discipline? The whole country, in fact – lack of structure? Lack of purpose?"

He leaned closer.

"… Lack of manliness?"

Cassandra was now both doubtful and confused.

"Well, yes, yes, now that you mention it, things do seem to be getting a bit squishy."

"Captain, did you know there is a culture that can supply that structure, that purpose… that manliness?"

"Well, I, uh… no, actually, no."

"I'm talking about Islam, Captain. Islam. Did you know that within one-hundred years of the Prophet's death, Islam conquered all of the Middle East? All of North Africa? Most of Spain? Biggest empire in the world! Pretty impressive, wouldn't you say?"

Cassandra grasped for a reply.

"Yes, yes, I see what you mean. That's certainly a good argument for Islam. Can't argue with success…"

When Cassandra first entered the office, General Panzer struck him as the kind of person who was thoroughly grounded in reality. It now occurred to him that the General might be thoroughly unhinged. Cassandra wondered if, like Captain Queeg in *The Caine Mutiny*, Panzer kept a set of large ball bearings in his desk to retrieve in times of stress and roll around in one of his massive hands. He decided on a different tack: he would try to appeal to whatever residual Christianity might still linger in the General's heart.

"Yes, Islam is an impressive faith all right. But still, this is a Christian nation, after all."

Panzer scowled.

"Christianity had its chance, Captain, and frankly, it blew it. Hitler understood that. You know what he said, Cassandra? He said "The Mohammedan religion would have been much more compatible to us than Christianity.

Why did it have to be Christianity with its meekness and flabbiness?"

"But Hitler was a racist. Wouldn't he have despised Muslims the same way he despised Jews?"

"That's where you're wrong. It's a common mistake to think of Islam as a race. But Islam's not a race, Captain, it's an idea – a very powerful idea. Here, let me show you something."

He reached into his desk drawer. Cassandra feared he might be reaching for the ball bearings, but instead he pulled out a framed photo.

"Do you know what this is? It's a photo of Hitler with the Grand Mufti of Jerusalem."

"The Grand…?"

"The Grand Mufti. He was the most important Islamic leader of the day."

He continued in a confiding tone.

"Now, not many people know this, but Hitler and the Mufti were close friends. They saw eye to eye. Together with Goebbels and Himmler they planned the final solution.

You see, they all understood where the real problem lay."

"The…real problem?"

"The Jews, Captain, the Jews. They were the problem then; they are the problem now. Why is this country weak and unmanly? It's the Jews. A very clever people, but not clever enough."

"Well, the, uh… unmanliness is certainly a problem, General. I'll grant you that. But I don't see how the Jews…" He trailed off, realizing that rational arguments were of no avail.

Panzer got up from his desk and circled around behind Cassandra. Leaning over the back of the Captain's chair he put a firm but comforting hand on his shoulder.

"I understand, Captain. It takes a while to get used to

a new idea. It took me a while to figure it out. But once you see all the pieces, it falls into place. Let me ask you, Cassandra: Where do you think the images of unmanliness come from?"

Cassandra smiled uneasily.

"Uh… well, I'm not sure…"

"They come from Hollywood, don't they?"

"Uh… yes… I suppose so, yes."

"And who controls Hollywood?"

Cassandra was having difficulty concentrating and the General's intimate hold on his shoulder only added to his discomfort. He began to rub his temples, trying to think.

"Uh… not sure…"

Panzer leaned closer.

"The Jews, Captain. They've got it in the palm of their hands. Do you follow me now?"

"Yes, yes, I can see what you mean…yes."

Cassandra chuckled nervously as he spoke and began to quietly laugh and cry. He couldn't manage, however, to control the shaking that now convulsed his body. He prayed that Panzer wouldn't notice.

CHAPTER 31

General Panzer stood up straight and moved around to face Cassandra. He squinted his eyes and silently studied him for a few moments.

"Captain, I take a certain pride in being able to size up a man, and I think you're the kind of man we could use in our organization. Is that something that would interest you, Captain?"

"Uh, well..."

He was afraid that if he said any more, his voice would betray his distress. In any event, he could think of nothing more to say.

Fortunately, Panzer was not paying much attention to Cassandra at that point. He was wrapped up in expounding on the rewards of his newfound faith.

"I think once you get to know what Islam is all about, you'll understand why I chose it. It's power, Cassandra, power to remake the world. But that's not all. There are other benefits, as well. You see, Allah really understands a man's needs. Four women for every man, Captain. Not a bad life, eh?"

He continued in a more philosophical vein.

"Of course, none of us knows how long he's going to live. But if you die fighting for Allah, you have quite a lot to look forward to in the next world."

He noticed that Cassandra did not seem enthused.

"What's the matter, Captain? I can see that something's bothering you. Perhaps it might help you to know that Allah understands that some men have different tastes. Rest assured, those tastes can be accommodated, too. Well, Captain, I'm offering you a big opportunity.

What do you say?"

Cassandra, who had regained some of his composure, spoke haltingly.

"Well, it's a very interesting offer. But... uh... very sudden. I'll, uh, need some time to think it over. Uh... why don't I get back to you in a few days?"

As he said this, he got up and edged toward the door.

"Not so fast, Captain. I need your answer now."

Cassandra realized that the game was up. He decided on a show of defiance.

"All right, then. You want to know what I say? I say you're off your rocker. You don't belong in the Pentagon, you belong in a nuthouse. Now, if you'll excuse me I'm going to walk down that hall to the office of the Joint Chiefs, and when I get there I am going to tell them all about you. And then you can try to explain your crackpot ideas to a military tribunal!"

He had intended to say this in a manner that would overawe the general, but his words came out at a slightly higher pitch than he had anticipated. Panzer did not appear to be overawed.

"I wouldn't do that if I were you, Captain."

He pressed a button on his desk and in stepped two muscular guards whose stylish black uniforms were reminiscent of the Nazi S.S. They seized Cassandra.

"Let... me... go! You... you'll regret this, General!" said Cassandra, struggling and sputtering.

"Relax, Captain. You're just going to pay a visit to Major Hussein. He's one of our top psychiatrists. Maybe he can cure you of your delusional thoughts. Major

Hussein?"

Major Hussein entered through another door in a wheelchair. He wore a doctor's white coat and a sinister smile.

"Come this way, Captain."

Accompanied by Major Hussein, the burly guards dragged Cassandra through the still-open door. A moment later, the General's aide entered from the other door.

"General, the car is waiting to take you to the president's press conference."

"Tell them I'll be there in a minute."

He picked up a red phone.

"Colonel, the press conference is set to begin in one hour. Are your men ready?... Good. You know when to give the order."

CHAPTER 32

President Prince made a point of being on time for the press conference. His nationalization of the dating services had alienated many young voters and his appointment of the rapper XYY as head of the National Endowment of the Arts had displeased some older members of the arts community, among who were some of his biggest contributors. More importantly, his national security policy had come under severe criticism in recent months. He thought it best not to alienate the members of the press any further by showing up late again – as he had at the last three briefings.

As the president took the podium, he nodded to General Panzer and Secretary Apoligeto, who were seated on either side. Then he addressed the members of the White House press corps who were seated facing him.

"I've called this press conference today to try to put to rest some concerns that have recently been raised about our national security. I've asked the Director of Homeland Security and one of the Pentagon's top strategists to join me. Secretary Apoligeto and General Panzer will be able to answer your more detailed questions about security and preparedness. So let's get started. Chip?"

Chip, who despite his youthful name appeared to be

at least fifty, rose and asked the first question.

"Mr. President, some of your critics have questioned your recent interim appointment of a devout Muslim as Assistant Secretary of Defense. Would you care to comment?"

"Let me just say that I have great confidence in Dr. Omar Saleem. He has served ably in my administration in several capacities and I'm sure he will bring a much-needed new perspective to the Defense Department. Now, let me say something else, Chip. I think that we have got to get beyond this idea that a Muslim can't serve his country as loyally and as ably as any other American citizen. We all know that there is a tiny minority of extremists who want to attack our way of life, and my advisors and I feel that the most effective way to combat those extremists is by bringing as many moderates as we can into mainstream positions – moderates like Dr. Saleem. Next question?... Taffy?"

Though young and perky in appearance, Taffy was all business.

"Mr. President, in regard to that tiny minority of extremists, would you care to comment on the recent attempted suicide bombings in New York, Chicago, and Anaheim? According to some sources, each of the would-be bombers was a devout Muslim."

"I'll turn that question over to Secretary Apoligeto," replied the president. "But before I do, I just want to caution the press not to jump to conclusions. We don't want to slander the beliefs of a billion and a half people on account of the actions of a few. Secretary Apoligeto?"

The president stood to one side and Secretary Apoligeto came over to the podium.

"Thank you, Mr. President and thank you, Taffy, for your question. I can assure you that this has nothing to do with Islam. These men were lone wolves acting on a warped understanding of their religion. Moreover, in each case there were obvious signs of mental or financial distress. Mr. Muhammad Musharaf, the suspect in the Radio City Music Hall attack was a recent immigrant from Pakistan who was apparently unable to adjust to the culture shock of living in New York City. Mr. Ismail Muhammad, the suspect in the Chicago case, had lost his job and was facing foreclosure on his house. And the third suspect, Mr. Muhammad Ahmed Muhammad, was deeply depressed following the sudden deaths of his wife and two daughters. These are normal, if somewhat unusual, responses to stressful situations. I think it does a great disservice to try and connect the acts of a few disturbed individuals to a great religion like Islam. Thank you."

"Thank you, Madam Secretary," said the president, who had moved back to the podium. He pointed to another member of the press. "Jake?"

"Mr. President, the Center for Security Research, a private think tank, has issued a report pointing to lax discipline in the military and a sharp drop-off in enlistments. Would you care to comment on this decline in enlistments coming at a time when other nations are building up their armies? Is our Army prepared to handle the rising threat level?"

"Jake, I'm going to turn your question over to General Panzer, but before I do, let me assure you that I have great confidence in our young men and women and… uh… transgendered folk who serve our country with bravery and distinction. And as far as numbers go, let me remind you of an old saying: 'It's not the size of the man in the fight, it's the size of the fight in the man.' Well, of course, nowadays, we wouldn't say 'man.' I'm just trying to make the point that when you're talking about our modern, highly trained military… er… size doesn't really matter. General?"

General Panzer took the podium. His commanding presence was complemented by the authoritative tone of his voice.

"Thank you, Mr. President. I'll be perfectly frank with you, Jake. There *has* been a loosening of discipline in our military. We are aware of that. Absence of discipline has always been a problem in the military. Even the Continental Army suffered from lax discipline. That's why General Washington called in von Steuben."

Von Steuben? A puzzled look crossed the president's face.

Panzer continued.

"Baron von Steuben knew a bit about discipline. He taught our boys to straighten up; he taught them to drill, and he taught them about submission."

Jake, Chip, Taffy, and other members of the press looked up from their notebooks. *Submission*?

"Gentlemen, he saved our army from itself. He was the one who forged an army at Valley Forge. Not many people know this but von Steuben is responsible for introducing the American soldier to the correct use of the bayonet. The Continental soldiers used it as a cooking tool. They thought it was for shish kebab. Well, the Baron knew better. He taught them how to *thrust* and *slash*. *Thrust* and *slash*, gentlemen, that's how you win wars."

The audience was now visibly disturbed.

"What else did he do? Well, you won't find this in the schoolbooks, but von Steuben established the standards of sanitation that have made our military the cleanest fighting force in the world."

He still spoke in an authoritative manner, but a certain strange quality had crept into his voice.

"Before his arrival, men relieved themselves where they wished, they...well, I'll leave that to your imaginations. Suffice it to say that the Baron cleaned up the filth. He laid out a plan of structured and orderly camps."

General Panzer paused at this point and then spoke more slowly and with great emphasis, as though what he was describing was a monumental breakthrough.

"Kitchens and latrines were on *opposite* sides of the camp and – and this was part of his genius – the latrines were built on the *downhill* side."

President Prince and Secretary Apoligeto exchanged worried glances. Panzer continued speaking, but now at a more rapid pace.

"Now, to answer your question: Is our Army prepared? The answer is that our Army is now rapidly preparing to rectify the lack of purpose, the lack of structure, and the lack of manliness that is endemic in our country. And I can personally assure you that right at this very moment, steps are being taken in bases across this land that will lead to significant and permanent improvements in discipline and order..."

CHAPTER 33

"Okay, that's the signal. Let's get started."

In the Muslim command center at Fort Camp, the officers had been intently watching a TV screen. When General Panzer uttered the words "bases across this land," Major Osama clicked off the TV and gave the order.

Moving quickly, the officers, with the help of three dozen enlisted men, broke open the weapons locker and passed assault rifles from hand to hand. They then dispersed in small groups across the base.

Their first objective was General Coddle. He was busy filing his nails when an officer and two soldiers burst into his office with pointed guns.

"You're under arrest, General." It was Captain Nasrallah and he obviously meant business.

General Coddle raised his hands in surrender.

"But, Abdul, Anwar – boys! There must be a misunderstanding. I'm sure we can change to a full halal menu, if that's the problem."

"There's no mistake, General. And halal isn't the problem. Now come with us."

"Well, if you insist, I won't try to stop you," said Coddle lamely.

"General, there's no way you can stop us now."

Meanwhile, similar scenes were being played out in more than half-a-dozen bases in the region. Commanding officers were arrested and replaced by Muslim officers, and Muslim soldiers simultaneously took command of weapon supplies and communication facilities. At a few of the bases, the rebel units encountered sporadic resistance, but they had the element of surprise and months of careful planning working in their favor. Within a few short hours, the Muslim forces had secured control of seven army bases.

Later that night in homes across the nation, TV viewers were suddenly confronted with a scene that might have come straight out of a James Bond thriller. Millions of TV screens went blank, only to be followed by a few moments of static. The next image to appear was that of a handsome officer seated at a desk behind which could be seen a flag with a crossed scimitar design. He was wearing the uniform of a U.S. Army Colonel.

"This is Colonel Mohammed Faisal speaking to you from the Islamic Command Center at Fort Camp, Virginia with a special alert. In the interest of the Nation's well-being and for the sake of its spiritual health, Muslim soldiers are now in the process of restoring honor to the Armed Services. Corrupt and degenerate officers are being purged from the ranks, and in their place, officers of piety and integrity will now serve. This is only the first step in the establishment of a new, honorable, and just order in America."

His hands were folded on the desk and he spoke calmly and sincerely, almost with a hint of regret that such action had become necessary.

"Our forces have taken command of seven army bases surrounding Washington. We possess enough chemical weapons to take the Capital by force, but we prefer a peaceful solution. We are now awaiting the president's reply to our demands. In the meantime, stay in your homes and you will not be harmed. Please do not be alarmed. All is now in Allah's hands. We invite all those who wish to do the will of the All-Merciful One to join our cause. Many of your fellow Americans are already rallying to our side. You will now be returned to your regular programming."

The screen went dark again, followed by static, and then back to whatever programs had been in progress.

Apparently, many of the broadcasters had been unaware that their programming had been appropriated for other purposes. On one channel, a reporter was reading the news off a teleprompter.

"...And so to recap the big news of the day, celebrity pop star Britney Bieber has been ordered to rehab after being sentenced for DUI. Fans of the mega-star – many of them accompanied by their parents – lined up outside the courthouse hoping to get a glimpse of their idol. Many carried signs saying 'We love you Britney,' and 'You're my BFF'... Well, that's it for tonight. Be sure to watch our one hour special report tomorrow at nine: 'Home School Hellholes.' Watch as our investigative reporters uncover the secret world of Christian home schooling – a world where children are actually forced to say grace and memorize scripture. You won't want to miss this one."

CHAPTER 34

When the nation awoke the next day, leftist, pro-Islamic rallies were already in progress on the National Mall. By noon Eastern Time, similar rallies had popped up in dozens of cities across the country. The demonstrators carried picture posters featuring Che Guevara, Lenin, and Osama Bin Laden. Hammer and sickle posters appeared side-by-side with crescent and star posters, and many of the activists held up signs on which the words "Power to the Prophet" were printed in bright red letters.

At the Mall, an enthusiastic TV reporter was describing the events.

"...And not just here in Washington, but all across cities in America – in New York, in Boston, in Chicago, and San Francisco – thousands have spontaneously taken to the streets in support of what is now being called "America's Arab Spring." People are literally dancing in the streets. And the sense of joy is contagious. You can feel the vibrations of happiness in the air as the good news spreads from group to group. I've covered a lot of demonstrations in my day, but I've never seen anything quite like this. What a day this has turned out to be!"

CHAPTER 35

Several miles from the Pentagon, in the security wing of a mental health facility, an orderly wheeled Captain Cassandra down a long corridor. Cassandra was straitjacketed and bound with straps to the wheelchair. He was extremely agitated. As they approached a nursing station, two female nurses looked up.

Cassandra saw this as his last chance to break through to the outside world. He would get hold of himself and speak to the nurses in a calm and reasonable voice. Once he had outlined the situation, they would see immediately that a mistake had been made, and while one was loosening his bonds, the other would get on the phone to alert the proper authorities, after which they would offer profuse apologies.

"Well, who do we have here?" asked one of the nurses.

"This is Jimmy," said the orderly. "He's a sad case. Thinks he's an army captain. The doctor says he's obsessed by conspiracy theories about a Muslim takeover of the whole world." The orderly spoke as though Cassandra were a toddler in a stroller whose own opinion of the matter was of little consequence.

This outrageous condescension had the effect of bringing all of Cassandra's pent-up emotions to the surface, and what he blurted out was not at all what he had intended to say.

"But there *is* a conspiracy! Please, you've got to listen to me! Please, please, just call the FBI. Tell 'em where I am. Tell them I've got the evidence! There's not much time!"

The nurses exchanged knowing glances with each other and with the orderly.

"See what I mean?" said the orderly, shrugging his shoulders. "Well, I got to take him down to the isolation ward. C'mon Jimmy, I'll take you to a nice quiet place."

He resumed wheeling Cassandra along the corridor. Cassandra struggled against his bonds and twisted his head back toward the nurses. With a wild look in his eye he shouted frantically at them.

"You've got to believe me! I *am* a captain! Call the FBI! Tell them! Tell the president! Call the Pentagon! No! Don't call the Pentagon…"

Still shouting, he was wheeled away.

CHAPTER 36

Later that day, President Prince addressed the nation on television from the East Room of the White House. To give the occasion an official stamp, a smattering of cabinet members and congressmen had been hastily assembled. The Vice President, the Senate Majority Leader, and the Speaker of the House were also present.

A translator for the deaf had been called in at the last minute to sign the speech. He was smooth-shaven but wore a long tan robe and a prayer cap. He looked like he was from Egypt or maybe Pakistan. The president couldn't tell the difference. To him, they all had pretty much the same Third-Worldish appearance.

President Prince had never understood why hand-signers were needed for such occasions. Why didn't people just get hearing aids or else turn up the volume on the TV, he wondered. In particular, he worried that the hand-signer's gestures would distract attention away from him.

The president's fears were well-founded. The interpreter seemed to have some ideas of his own about speech-making. Before the talk was half a minute along, he began to add his own editorial gestures.

The president started on a confident note.

"Yesterday, as you know, our nation stood on the

brink of civil war. Today, I am pleased to report that we have pulled back from that brink. To prevent further bloodshed, my administration has agreed to share power with Muslim military and political leaders."

At this point, the hand-signer nodded in agreement and made a thumbs-up gesture.

The president continued.

"In the coming days you will be told the full details of this new arrangement which, we believe, will best serve the interests of our great nation. At this point I can only assure you that both sides have made significant concessions for the good of the country. For many of you, this will be a difficult adjustment. But we must remember that America's foremost commitment is, and always has been, to change. And I feel confident that, as the days go by, we as a nation will discover that this is the change we have been waiting for."

This too met with the signer's approval and he nodded vigorously.

"Why is this change needed now? For too long, our Muslim neighbors have suffered under a burden of suspicion and of second-class citizenship. To make up for past injustice, we must bring our Muslim citizens into full participation in the affairs of government. Let us never forget the debt we owe to Islamic-Americans."

As the president reminded Americans of the debt they owned to Muslims, the translator jabbed his index finger at the camera, much as the president himself often did when emphasizing a point. In fact, President Prince was just about to make that very gesture when he glimpsed the signer out of the corner of his eye. The interpreter seemed to be taking liberties with his speech. The president hoped this wasn't going to be a repeat of an incident that had happened a few years before at the funeral of Nelson Mandela. The man who had landed the hand-signing assignment for that occasion turned out to be a complete fake. His signs had been nothing but nonsense gestures. All of the dignitaries' carefully prepared talks had been rendered into tales told by idiots, signifying nothing. Ever since then, world leaders had taken pains to be sure that interpreters for the deaf were carefully vetted. Still, no system was foolproof. Had another kook managed to slip under the radar?

These thoughts passed through the president's brain in less than two seconds. He concentrated again on the teleprompter. Where was he? Oh, yes.

"Let us not forget the brave Muslims who fought at Valley Forge, who helped to draft our Bill of Rights, who fought at Shiloh and Gettysburg to end slavery, and who marched in Selma, Alabama to bring civil rights to blacks. Now it is time for Islamic-Americans to share in those same rights – time for America to do the right thing. As we know from the Holy Koran, God is all-merciful and all compassionate, and he will reward those who do good deeds with shaded gardens in paradise and, above all, with shapely companions graced with eternal youth..."

When the president described paradise, his eyes took on a dreamy look. The look in the translator's eyes was of a more naughty nature. For the benefit of the less imaginative in the audience, he traced an hourglass figure in the air.

President Prince pulled himself out of his paradisiacal reverie and came down to earth again.

"...Er, but let us not think only of eternal rewards. Let us think also of the many immediate benefits that the American people will derive from this new spirit of cooperation and mutual respect. As you know, a spiritual void has developed in America – a lack of purpose that has resulted in a lack of structure, a lack of discipline, and... er... a lack of manliness."

This part of the speech had been inserted by General Panzer. It wasn't exactly the way the president would have put it, but under the circumstances he had seen no sense in quibbling.

"I know that I speak for a growing number of Americans who now believe that there is only one spiritual force that can fill that void, and restore the direction and manliness that our society lacks."

As he paused to let his words sink in, the hand signer raised both hands in a victory sign.

Prince was pleased with himself. He felt he had hit all the right notes. The Islamists would be pleased with the spiritual overtones. Ordinary Americans would be reassured that what looked like a *coup d' etat* was merely the logical outgrowth of traditional American values and aspirations. He wouldn't be surprised if his words would be looked upon by future historians as epochal – a grand gesture of reconciliation that healed wounds and bridged divisions. Yes, he had surpassed himself. It was even better than his last acceptance speech. In a sense, it *was* an acceptance speech. The Islamist leaders had agreed to let him stay on as president so as to provide an appearance of continuity. There were certain conditions attached to the offer, of course, but he thought them not at all unreasonable.

With his jaw tilted at what he thought was just the right angle, he continued.

"Let us recall that one of the great, but often neglected principles of our founding is submission to authority. And this is a value that we share in common with Islam. The genius of Islam is that it shows us how to find peace through submission."

At this the hand-signer adopted a prayerful pose.

"Now, as a gesture of goodwill, I plan to lead by example in this regard. In submission to the will of the All-Merciful One, I have appointed a commission tasked with finding two suitable young women for me to marry in accordance with Islamic tradition. Naturally, this will in no way affect my relationship with my current wife, Rochelle, who has graciously consented to the new arrangement."

Amazed by the president's audacity, the translator

stopped signing altogether and simply stared at him in wide-eyed awe.

"She will, of course, remain as First Lady, with my new wives serving as Second Lady and Third Lady. Unfortunately, our dog, Lady, will have to go to the pound out of deference to traditional Muslim sensibilities about the canine species."

The hand-signer resumed signing – more rapidly now in order to catch up.

"I will add that many members of the Congress have expressed great interest in joining me in this gesture of submission by seeking additional wives of their own. Moreover, our newly formed unity government has pledged to quickly enact specific legislation to reflect these new realities. We have proposed, and we expect a speedy passage of a new law – The Defense of Multiple Marriages Act. This law is designed to protect a man's right to domestic tranquility, and… er, spousal variety."

The hand-signer rubbed his hands in a gesture of gleeful anticipation.

The president's conclusion was both upbeat and reassuring.

"In conclusion, let me re-emphasize that, because of the efforts of good men on both sides, we have managed to avoid a costly and unnecessary war. Instead, we have achieved peace – an honorable peace for which future generations will thank us. As the prophet Jesus, peace be upon him, said, 'Blessed are the peacemakers.' Our children and our children's children will thank us for this peaceful resolution… Thank you."

The interpreter wiped his brow in relief, thankful that the speech had finally ended.

CHAPTER 37

The next day, a small reception was held in the Oval Office of the White House to celebrate the peaceful transition.

The Oval Office had undergone a transformation of its own. Gone was the large circular rug with the eagle emblem. In its place was a circular green rug carrying the now- familiar crossed scimitar and book design. Frederic Remington's *Bronco Buster* statuette had been removed from the desk to make way for a statue of Saladin the Great mounted on a warhorse. Washington's portrait remained on the wall but was now accompanied by portraits of Marx, Lenin, and Mohamed Morsi. The bust of Lincoln on the mantle had been replaced with a bust of Osama bin Laden.

A small buffet had been set up, and something like a cocktail party was in progress, except that no alcoholic beverages were available, only tea, soft drinks, fruit juices, and some sort of camel milk concoction flavored with honey. The atmosphere was, nevertheless, convivial.

Among the guests were members of the president's security council, several senators, a handful of Muslim officers, some bearded Muslim gentlemen, and a few members of the press. In one corner of the room, a small group was gathered around General Panzer. Jennifer Apoligeto was in the middle of complimenting him.

"Isn't it so exciting?! And you played such an important role."

"All in the line of duty, ma'am. All in the line of duty," said Panzer, who was in the process of lighting a cigar.

The secretary signaled to an admiral in a white dress uniform.

"Oh, waiter, could you bring some more of these delicious hors d'oeuvres?"

The admiral, for whatever reason, decided to play the role of a waiter.

"Certainly, ma'am" he replied in his best waiter's voice, and went off to locate the hors d'oeuvres.

"That's a rear admiral, Madam Secretary," said General Panzer.

Apoligeto put her hand to her mouth in a gesture of embarrassment.

"Oh, my!"

A portly, balding man, who seemed eager to get in on the conversation, took this opportunity to add his own compliments to the several that Panzer had already received.

"General, I just wanted to thank you for your role in putting down this Zionist conspiracy. I've been warning my colleagues about them for ages. Tell me, is it true that you've been put in charge of the invasion of Israel?"

"Don't believe all the rumors you hear, Senator… what's the last name, again?"

"Goldberg. Senator Reuben Goldberg," said the senator with a hint of pride in his voice.

Panzer clamped down on his cigar and scowled.

"Goldberg… hmm, that's a Jewish name, isn't it?"

In another part of the room, Senator Franky Barnstable was in conversation with Colonel Faisal and Major Osama.

"Gentlemen, you deserve the countwy's thanks for a

bwilliant wescue opewation. If it wasn't for you, this countwy might have fallen into the hands of wight-wing extwemists. If there is anything I can do, please let me know."

"Anything you can do?" replied the Colonel smoothly. "Why, yes. The Major and I want to have our picture taken together. I have a camera in my briefcase. Perhaps you could take our picture?"

"I would be gwad to."

"Not right now, of course. After the ceremonies. Perhaps up on the roof? – with the monument in the background." He gave Osama a knowing glance.

"On the woof? Of course. That's a spwendid idea."

In another part of the room, two middle-aged women wearing token scarves were in conversation. Senator Rose Smith, the senator from South Carolina, was excitedly sharing the latest gossip with her companion.

"Oh my, it was simply shocking! It was on the news last night. He was the leader of a Mormon sect. Seven wives, and three of them were only fourteen! They sentenced him to twenty years. Good riddance! What a horrible man!"

As they chattered on about Mormon malfeasance, an older man in a dark suit approached them. With him was a bearded, middle-aged man dressed in a Bedouin robe and a keffiyeh. He wore a heavy gold medallion on a chain around his neck and a large gold ring on his finger. Accompanying him were two teenaged girls in chadors which covered everything except their faces. Even with the chador it was obvious that they were quite young.

"Senator Smith. Let me introduce Sheik Hafaz," said the older man. "He asked to meet you."

"Good afternoon, Senator, it's a pleasure to meet you. You have been a good friend to my country." The sheik spoke with a pronounced accent.

Senator Smith gushed in reply.

"Well, thank you. It's a pleasure to meet you, too. I've

heard so much about you. And these two lovely girls must be your daughters?"

The older man cleared his throat.

"Oh, no," replied the sheik. "These are my wives – two of them. The others are at home. This is Sabrina and this is Jasmine."

The girls smiled and nodded.

"Oh, yes, of course – that's part of your culture. I'd forgotten. Well, they are very charming young women."

"Oh, they are not so young anymore," admitted the sheik. "Sabrina here will have her braces off next year. Show the lady your braces, Sabrina."

Sabrina bent down to lift the hem of her ankle-length chador. She was interrupted by a sharp order from her husband.

"Not those braces!"

Realizing her mistake, Sabrina straightened up, and smiled broadly, revealing the braces on her teeth.

Senator Smith gushed again.

"What a delightful smile! Sheik, you and your dau... your wives must come and visit my husband and I at our home. We'd love to have you."

Meanwhile, in another part of the room, a group of reporters were clustered around the president. Casey and Emerson were among them, only now Casey wore a hijab and Emerson had the beginnings of a beard on his chin. Their conversation was interrupted by an aide, who came up to the president and whispered in his ear.

The president made his apologies to the reporters.

"That's all the questions for now. I've just been informed that the Saudi ambassador has arrived. Ah! There he is."

The Saudi ambassador entered, dressed in traditional Saudi robes and head covering. The president bowed low to him, then the two exchanged the traditional Muslim greeting, "Assalamu alaykum."

"Greetings, brother. I hope I find you in good health.

The King sends his greetings and good wishes, and says that he hopes you can soon visit him in Mecca."

The ambassador spoke in ambassador-ese and the president replied in kind.

"Thank you, that is most gracious of the King. If it pleases His Majesty, I will arrange to come at the next pilgrimage."

"He will be most pleased. In the meantime, he has asked me to give you this token of his esteem."

An aide to the ambassador handed him a scimitar in a jeweled scabbard, and the ambassador then presented it to the president.

"I am most honored. Please thank His Majesty for me."

"Of course it is for ceremonial purposes only," winked the ambassador. "As you know, we are a peaceful people."

"Of course," replied the president knowingly.

The aide to the president interrupted with another whispered message.

"Excuse me, Mr. Ambassador," apologized the president. "I have just been reminded that it is time for prayer."

At this point the women obligingly left the room while the men gathered up prayer rugs that were stacked in a pile near the large south-facing windows. There was some confusion at first about the placement of the rugs. Three bearded men began to argue among themselves in loud voices.

"But in which direction do we kneel?" demanded the first.

The second man pointed toward the windows, and spoke impatiently.

"This is the West Wing, so Mecca must be in the opposite direction – over there."

The third man was incensed.

"No! No! If this is the West Wing, then east is over

there!" He pointed in another direction.

"I tell you, it is this way!" said the second angrily.

The third man put his hand on the hilt of his dagger.

"By Allah! You blaspheme!"

President Prince who had noticed the commotion, signaled with his hands for them to calm down.

"Gentlemen! Gentlemen! Please restrain yourselves. The direction of Mecca is indicated by the arrow on the wall."

He pointed to a green arrow painted on the wall.

"Let us conduct ourselves peacefully, as our Prophet, peace be upon him, has commanded."

The three men nodded grudgingly and threw down their prayer rugs in the direction of the arrow. Within half a minute, all present were kneeling toward Mecca.

CHAPTER 38

Outside, the light was beginning to fade, and long shadows lay across the White House lawn. A Marine honor guard had ascended to the roof in order to change flags. They saluted Colonel Faisal and Major Osama, but didn't think to wonder what the two officers were doing on the White House roof or why they had been peering over the side at the lawn below.

To the beat of a drum, a Marine lowered the American flag and raised a green flag with a crescent and star to the top of the White House flag pole. As the flag fluttered in the breeze, a bearded marine played "taps" on his trumpet. From that height, the melancholy sound carried far out over the National Mall.

From somewhere off in the distance another sound could be heard. A marching band, apparently ill-informed about the new order of things, was practicing the "Stars and Stripes Forever." They played the rousing piece with gusto, but not loudly enough to offset the chilly silence that had begun to descend on Washington.

CHAPTER 39

Neither sound could be heard in the small windowless room of the isolation ward which had become Captain Cassandra's new residence. It was not isolation in the strict sense, since Cassandra received the full attention of the hospital staff. But he was not yet allowed to mingle with the other patients for fear of what the nurses called "thought contamination."

He had been diagnosed as suffering from acute Islamophobia accompanied by episodes of paranoid ideation. Nevertheless, his doctor was confident that he would make a full recovery provided he stuck to the prescribed therapeutic regime. Dr. Zakaria was a dark-skinned Pakistani with a prominent prayer bump in the middle of his forehead. He had recently transferred from England – or, as it was now called due to the events of the last 72 hours, the Islamic Republic of England. Dr. Z, as he liked to be called, laughed every time he forgot himself and used the old designation. Cassandra, he insisted, should also try to break his old thought patterns and develop new ones. "It takes a while to get used to a new idea," he said, "but life will become happier for you."

It was true, thought Cassandra, that Dr. Z was a happy man, or seemed to be. The Muslim nurses who attended him also seemed happy. They always smiled as they went about their routines, and they looked quite becoming in their modest but stylish hijabs.

One of the nurses told him that he was lucky because Dr. Z had been trained in Koranotherapy, which had proven to be a very effective rehabilitation technique in European clinical trials. Indeed, Cassandra had been provided with a copy of the Koran – the Yusuf Ali translation, which, according to the same nurse, was renowned for its therapeutic effects. He was to read a chapter each day. "A chapter a day keeps the doctor away." Dr. Z had said this jokingly, but Cassandra could see that he really believed it.

Next to the Koran on his table lay a printed schedule outlining his therapeutic regimen for the coming week. Besides the daily Koran reading, there would be short videos, cultural awareness sessions provided by the Unitarian Universalist Church (which had recently merged with that much larger Unitarian church headquartered in Mecca), group therapy, Arabic calligraphy (which he supposed was the Islamic version of art therapy), and Friday prayer service at the hospital mosque (voluntary). In addition, he would receive twice-weekly lessons in the "essentials of Islam." Tomorrow he would be visited by the hospital chaplain – an imam – for his first lesson.

Cassandra was determined he would never succumb to the conditioning process, let them try their damnedest. He had taken a vow to uphold the Constitution and, even if he had not, he was not going to betray his country and what it stood for. Moreover, seventy-two virgins or not, he would never consider conversion to this alien faith. He had stopped practicing his own faith years before, but he had not stopped believing in it. No, he would not give in, even if he were the last American to hold out.

At times, however, he found himself thinking how much easier it would be to simply submit.

ABOUT THE AUTHOR

William Kilpatrick is the author of several books about cultural and religious issues, including *Psychological Seduction, Why Johnny Can't Tell Right From Wrong* and, most recently, *Christianity, Islam and Atheism: The Struggle for the Soul of the West*.

Kilpatrick's articles on cultural and educational topics have appeared in *First Things, Policy Review, American Enterprise, American Educator, Los Angeles Times*, and various scholarly journals. His articles on Islam have appeared in *Investor's Business Daily, FrontPage Magazine, JihadWatch, Crisis, Catholic World Report, New Oxford Review,* and other publications.

Insecurity, his first novel, was born of his interest in the West's politically correct kowtowing to Islam.

"The West's capitulation to the tyranny of diversity is disturbing," says Kilpatrick, "but it also has its comic side. In writing *Insecurity*, I had a difficult time inventing situations that were any more absurd than the ones being reported with a straight face on the daily news."

CPSIA information can be obtained at www.ICGtesting.com
Printed in the USA
BVOW05s2144210714

360007BV00001B/8/P

9 781618 689436